NOBODY'S HERO
A SHORT STORY COLLECTION

MARK LESLIE

STARK
PUBLISHING

Table of Contents

Stark Publishing
January 2021

eBook: 978-1-989351-10-9

Paperback: 978-1-989351-09-3

Audiobook: 978-1-989351-11-6

The characters and events portrayed in this short story collection are fictitious. Any similarity to real persons, living or dead, is coincidental and not intended by the author. (Except for at least one of the strangers killed in "Collateral Damage" who might be based upon a real person. But you can read about that in the post-story notes)

Visit Mark Leslie on the web at www.markleslie.ca[1]

Follow Mark on Twitter @MarkLeslie[2]

Sign up for Mark Leslie's newsletter[3] to receive a free eBook.

---

1. http://www.markleslie.ca
2. https://twitter.com/markleslie
3. http://markleslie.us4.list-manage.com/subscribe?u=ed5625948004c11696c7313a3&id=f9caf5a705

Dedication

For Neil Peart (Sept 12, 1952 to Jan 7, 2020).
With thanks for a lifetime of inspiration in music and words.

Introduction

What makes a hero?

Is a hero someone who puts on a mask and costume and rushes to the rescue to save the day? Is a hero someone whose exploits results in the discovery of a miraculous cure to a life-threatening disease or plague? Is a hero someone who employs their supernatural ability for good and to assist others? Is a hero someone who loves another person or a cause so much that they risk life and limb in order to protect or save them from peril? Is a hero someone who stops in the midst of hustle and bustle to listen to those who no longer have a voice?

All of those things, can, of course, make a hero.

Heroes come in all kinds of shapes, sizes, and personas.

Saving the world can come in an epic and dramatic, world-shattering event; but it often can happen in small ways, in the one-on-one interactions people have with one another; in the subtle ways one small action can have a dramatic impact.

The stories you are about to read are all about heroes. Some of them are vigilante justice warriors. Some are accidental heroes caught between a tough situation and the choices they have to make. Some are just those who are living their lives in ways that subtly, and, positively affect others. And some are folks who are merely brave in the face of darkness and horrifying circumstances.

Some Are Born to Save the World is the tale of a man who has dedicated his entire life to using his supernatural abilities to fighting bad guys as a superhero. What happens when he reaches an age where his powers and his body have weathered away and can no longer support his desire to leap the proverbial tall building in a single bound?

Collateral Damage concerns itself with an accidental vigilante whose death curse can be used to help; even if that help sometimes comes with unexpected and undesired side-effects.

The main character in *The Zombie Whisperer* is another accidental hero, a red-neck "good old boy" whose thirst for adventure and danger leads to an unexpected benefit nobody ever imagined.

In *This Time Around* we follow a "day in the life" of a man afflicted with a werewolf curse who, while dealing with the side effects of lycanthropy, can't help but to use his heightened senses and strength to assist others he encounters, even if it means delaying his forward momentum.

The end of the world can come more like a whimper than a scream, as you'll read about in *A Murder of Scarecrows*. In this tale, another unlikely hero is less concerned with the rest of the world, and more worried about the only woman he has ever loved.

From Out of the Night is a tale that explores one woman's valiant attempt to face her fears head-on in order to protect her family from the terrors that stalk her home and family.

And, finally, *Memento Mori* is a cautionary tale about the short-sightedness in which we have become accustomed in the hustle and bustle of the modern world.

This collection was originally compiled from among the hundred or so short stories and novellas I have previously published in magazines, collections, and anthologies, specifically drawn together for a themed StoryBundle called *Saving the World* that Dean Wesley Smith invited me to be a part of in the late fall of 2019.

That particular bundle was only available for a limited time, and so, I tweaked the eBook, changed the title, and made a few revisions to it, particularly because I thought the theme and these stories might be enjoyed as a stand-alone story collection.

In early January of 2020, as I was finishing up work on an editing project, and has been reflecting on a story co-authored by Kevin J. Anderson and Neil Peart that I was reprinting, I ended up deciding on a new title for the self-release of the collection. The title was inspired by the song "Nobody's Hero" by the Canadian progressive rock band,

RUSH. I have, admittedly, been a huge fan of the band since the early 1980's, and much of my writing over the years has been influenced by their music and their lyrics. This particular song, which was from the 1993 RUSH album *Counterparts* and was written by drummer and lyricist Neil Peart, is a beautiful exploration of the everyday people who do brave and heroic things and yet are never thought of as heroes.

The first verse of the song explores Peart's friendship to a homosexual man who died of AIDS in the late '80s. The second verse talks about the brutal murder of a young woman from Peart's hometown. Considering where he grew up, I can only imagine that he was referring to Kristen French, who was abducted, tortured and murdered by serial killer Paul Bernardo.

I thought that the title Peart had selected for this song would be perfect for the collection I had put together.

Little did I know that Peart had died around the same time I had come to that conclusion.

Peart died from an aggressive form of brain cancer (glioblastoma), on January 7, 2020, in Santa Monica, California. He had been diagnosed three and a half years earlier, shortly after he had retired from touring with RUSH in order to spend more time focusing on his family and enjoying writing. Peart's illness was kept strictly secret among his family and closest friends. Though he died on Tuesday, January 7th, the official announcement of his death didn't even come until Friday January 10th, a simple matter of trying to keep it as low key as possible out of respect for the family. Peart had long been a private man and had never been comfortable with fame and the odd form of celebrity that came with that. He was content with working hard at something he was passionate about and didn't understand why people needed to hold celebrities in such high regard or want to be close with them. In fact, in the song "Limelight" he revealed through his lyrics that he was "ill-equipped" to handle such fame and that it was difficult for him to pretend that a person he had never met could be a "long-awaited friend."

Despite the plan to keep the news cycle of Peart's death low, fans and fellow musicians from around the world both lamented the man's loss and paid tribute to his incredible talent, his humble nature, and the way that he had inspired them.

I'm writing these words as I am sipping on a glass of *The Macallan*, Neil's favorite scotch, and I am thinking about how the man's own writing and music inspired me for most of my life.

It is fitting, then, that the book is dedicated to Neil Peart. Because, like he writes about in the song "Nobodys' Hero" when I heard that he was gone, I felt a shadow cross my heart.

The tales you are about to read are perhaps best described as being similar to the types of stories you might encounter in a *The Twilight Zone, The Outer Limits*, or *Amazing Stories* episode. If you're not of a certain age like me you'll likely only know these old television shows via repeats and YouTube clips. You might liken the tales to something you may see on an episode of *Black Mirror* – only, my stories tend to involve less of the science-fiction element on that program and a lot more of the eerie and supernatural.

I go into a bit more detail, and I provide *stories-behind-the-stories* for each of the tales, in a short section at the end of this book. That's where I'll reveal to you some insights behind the inspiration of the writing of each tale, as well as other insights I think you might enjoy. That is, only if you're one who enjoys those behind-the-scene tales.

If you're not into that, then you're likely better off just skipping that part and enjoying the stories on their own.

But, in the meantime, let's get into the stories.

And let's see how these characters, in their own way, are nobody's hero, despite the things that they do to try to save the world, or help others, one small action at a time.

Mark Leslie
January 2020

Some Are Born to Save The World

With all of the strength left in him, Bryan lifted his arm and extended his hand.

His knuckles cracked as his fingers stretched to their limits. But he was still half an inch shy of his mark.

"I won't go down this way!" tears of rage streaked down his face as he wheezed in an exhalation of stale, dry air that burned both his lungs and his throat. "White Vector will not die today!"

Despite the futility of his situation, he wouldn't give up.

He had simply come too far.

* * *

As a young child, Bryan spent more than his fair share of time cowering in the dark while listening to the sounds of his drunken father beating on his mother and calling her a useless, lazy bitch.

His father hated his life and took it out on his wife, since Bryan's mother always ensured, when Daniel Rand got into those moods, that Bryan was hidden away.

He was a scrawny child and easily frightened. And lying there in the dark under the bed or in a nearby closet, he kept wondering if he might ever grow big enough, or strong enough, or brave enough to stand up to his father and save his mother from the pain and humiliation.

He did his best to cover his ears so he couldn't hear the sound of fists hitting flesh nor his mother's cries of pain. To drown out the slaps and punches and cries, he replayed stories from the comic books he constantly escaped into, stories driven by truth, justice and the American way. He dreamed of one day being able to stop bad people from harming good people.

Especially his mother.

The supernatural powers he had dreamed about began manifesting themselves when he was mid-way through puberty. It was during the times when he had laid in the dark listening to the horrible sounds and kept thinking as hard as he could and with all of his might, that he wished his father would just leave them, would just pick up and leave, never to return.

One night, those feelings burning within him, Bryan stepped out of his hiding place and stood quietly looking at his father.

His old man turned, spittle running down his chin from the curses that accompanied each strike of his fist. The burning hatred in his father's eyes was clear and Bryan tensed, waiting for the attack — but it never came. His father merely stared him down while the rage seemed to deflate right out of him. As he watched the heated anger fade from the man's eyes, Bryan felt a confidence flowing within, a boundless sense of energy and strength.

"Enough!" Bryan said, expelling the word and the energy he felt pent up inside.

As if to punctuate his word, the dome and light bulb in the ceiling above his head exploded.

Without saying a word, Bryan's father looked at his son, the broken light fixture, his unconscious wife, and then back to his son. He made a move as if to step forward, but stopped, almost as if something invisible was preventing his progress.

More than anything, Bryan wished that his father would just go away, just leave.

After a minute of silent staring, his father turned, walked out the front door and disappeared into the night never to return.

It took several days of pondering the scene before Bryan realized the power that must have existed within him. It wasn't immediately apparent, because the force-flow of power had appeared in odd fits and starts — the way acne would appear without warning, or his pre-pubescent voice would crack at random. By his early twenties he had mastered the odd ability to focus and channel ambient energy life force from his body and from those around him either into himself, providing super-human strength, dexterity, and agility, or to affect objects with a telekinetic-like power. He would never be meek and helpless again.

* * *

Bryan tried to take in a deep breath, but he might as well have been sucking a mouthful of crackers into his lungs for all the good it did. The breath of air was devoid of the vital oxygen his body needed.

He was out of oxygen and, sadly, almost out of time.

But he had gotten out of life and death struggles before.

Hundreds of them.

White Vector was, after all, the people's hero who had always found a way.

This is no different than that day on the bridge, he thought.

* * *

It was a stifling hot summer day when he had first donned the white skin-tight costume with the crimson shorts and the vector-based, round four-color swirl on his chest, the red leather boots and the red hooded mask.

After several years of carefully planning out his costume, his name, and exactly how he could put them to use, he was about to step out into public prepared to change into his alter ego: White Vector.

That July afternoon, wearing the outfit under his street clothes, the hood tucked into his knapsack, was a day he had ultimately been needed.

He didn't have the ability to fly like Superman, nor to scale walls or swing from building to building like Spider-Man, nor even to race through the city streets in a super slick Batmobile like Batman, so public transit was the quickest way to get about the city. He got around by bus, subway, or train.

He had been riding the Q60 bus from Queens to Manhattan when a transport truck blew a tire and drove a station wagon up against the guard rails with such force that it crashed through, the back half of the car dangling precariously over the edge.

After taking a quick visual survey to ensure his passengers were physically unharmed after the sudden stop, the bus driver opened the doors and ran toward the station wagon.

Bryan took that moment to slip outside, pulling his backpack off while ducking below the bus windows and behind the steel wall of the transport truck. There, he pulled the hooded mask over his head and then quickly removed his shirt and pants and stuffed them into his knapsack before tossing it under the transport.

He wondered if he'd ever get those street clothes back: it never seemed to be an issue where Peter Parker or Clark Kent stashed their civvies.

In his mostly white and red costume, Bryan — now transformed into White Vector — walked back around the front of the bus and watched the bus driver finish pulling the male driver and female passenger out of the station wagon.

The driver had a bleeding gash on his forehead and was stumbling away from the car, looking dazed. The passenger, who seemed uninjured, was turning back to the car as if she wanted to climb back in, but the bus driver held her by the arm.

"My baby!" she cried. "He's in the back. In his car seat."

The car, though, was teetering, slowly rocking, looking as if any sort of extra weight on it would send it plummeting down into the river.

"Don't worry, ma'am!" Bryan said, stepping between the woman and the car. "I'm White Vector. And I'm here to help. What's his name?"

"Bobby."

"Stand back, please! It's going to be okay." Bryan said, then turned toward the car. "It's okay, Bobby! I've got you. You'll be safe."

The front of the car was pitched up almost two feet in the air in its teeter, and Bryan grabbed onto the steel bumper and let the power that flowed through the blood in his veins become an extremely focused concentration of strength into his arms and upper body. He also siphoned slivers of strength from those nearby. Each power siphon didn't last more than a minute or two, but it was often enough for him to perform some superhuman activity.

He pulled at the car's bumper, and the entire vehicle began to slowly slide back onto the bridge, one inch, then two.

"Oh my god!" someone shouted. "He's lifting the car!"

With a wail of scraping metal, the bumper Bryan was holding was no longer attached to the front of the car. The vehicle slid back quickly, farther back than it had been sitting before.

The car was now dangling at a nearly ninety-degree angle to the bridge, and, inside, Bobby was wailing even louder for his mommy.

"Do something!" Bobby's mother screamed.

Bryan shuffled over to the side nearest the open door, dropped down onto the pavement, and peered through the triangle of space between the car, the door, and the edge of the bridge. He couldn't climb into the car because the extra weight would send it toppling down. But he wondered if he might be able to lie on the bridge, stretch his upper body inside the car, and grab the child and pull him to safety.

Inching his way forward, he finally got to a point where he could lean most of his upper body into the car without putting any of his weight on the vehicle. He reached down past the back of the driver's seat toward the car seat. The only sounds, besides the wind, were Bobby's cries and the gentle creaking of the car as it continued to shift and rock.

With his arm fully extended, he was still a good three inches away from reaching the buckle. The child, who looked to be less than two years old, was crying harder and louder than before.

"Damn," Bryan muttered. His arm just didn't reach far enough.

But my mind can.

Bryan took a deep breath, concentrated on the unseen energy flowing through his body, on the anxious energy pumping out of Bobby's mother, the bus driver, and even the nearby passengers from the bus. He could feel their life force and drew strings of it into his mind, wrapping it into a tight ball.

Then, with a focus that completely blocked everything else out, Bryan propelled the ball forward in a pencil thin compacted blast of air.

The force was enough to depress the buckle.

Pop.

The straps on either side of the buckle released.

Bryan's head immediately filled with a lightning burst of white-hot pain, and it took everything in him not to yell out or move his body in any way that would touch the vehicle.

Now the hard part.

Bryan drew in more energy and channeled it down through his extended arm. He could feel the mystical power throbbing through his arm, and he pushed out an energy field that wrapped around the toddler's body.

When he felt the child securely within his grasp, his mind pulled back and up, and the toddler levitated forward up and out of the car seat toward Bryan as if by unseen hands.

The pressure in his head grew to a pounding series of quakes,

and he could feel the blood vessels in his nose bursting.

Blood trickled down his chin and splashed onto the toddler's face as he telekinetically pulled Bobby up close enough to grab a handful of the toddler's shirt and finish pulling him the rest of the way up. Wailing, Bobby grabbed at Bryan's forearm and held on as he was slowly lifted up.

Bobby's shoulders cleared the window, the toddler kicked out and hit the steering wheel with his knee.

The car teetered at a much sharper angle.

Bryan pulled the child in and as close to his chest as he could, shielding the boy's body while the car pitched forward, finally breaking free of the tentative hold the bridge and railing had on it and plummeting into the cold waters more than a hundred feet below.

Bryan felt his energy leaving him, a side-effect he recognized that came immediately after he drew in and expended such a burst of energy. He could just manage to roll onto his back to present the screaming toddler to his mother.

Not a bad first public use of his powers.

* * *

It would be just like that child on the Queensboro Bridge, Bryan thought, reaching his arm as far forward.

He was so close; but it was just out of reach, and the lack of breath was causing a tightness in his chest.

He tried channeling what little energy he could gather from his ailing body into the end of his right arm like he had done that first time he had played at super hero.

But the power wouldn't flow.

It wasn't like before.

Ever since his stroke, the one that had incapacitated his left side, he had been unable to get the energy, the power to flow anywhere near his left side. It was as if that part of his supernatural powers had died somewhere as an even more critical side effect.

He had, of course, seen the degeneration coming well before the stroke had hit.

Understanding enough about physics, Bryan knew that for every action there was an equal and opposite reaction. For the force to flow he knew the energy had to come from somewhere. He just had never properly counted the ultimate cost to playing hero for so many years.

***

The plane was headed for a crash course into the side of the Goldman Sachs building in the Paulus Hook neighborhood and there was nothing anybody could do about it. A freak accident during takeoff involving a series of birds striking both engines and causing them to fail created a scenario so oddly similar to the one in early 2009.

Only, in this case, the pilot wasn't able to get the plane on course for a relatively safe landing in the Hudson. There simply wasn't enough power.

Bryan had been on the Staten Island Ferry when the plane started to go down, and, along with his fellow New Yorkers, had been stunned to see a plane coming in so low over the city. It was impossible to see such a sight and not immediately think about that September day in 2001.

It was a rush-hour ferry, and as Bryan stood in the crowd of commuters, watching the plane swoop down, he reached out and grasped at the tentacles of energy from the thousands of fellow passengers, quickly and subtly pulling just a little bit of life force from each of them.

He channeled the gathered mass of energy and reached out to try to gently push the plane slightly off of its crash course into the tall office tower. His head rumbled with the force of concentration and the distance involved in manipulating the force as he grasped onto the rail of the passenger ferry. But he managed to nudge it just enough so it didn't strike the side of the building and then, body quivering, guided the plane down for a landing in the cold and choppy waters of the Hudson River.

The plane splashed down with the nose pointed down, and it must have immediately begun taking on water.

Exhausted and actually weeping from the throbbing pain in his head, Bryan began to again channel fragments of power from those around him and funneled it into another mass. With the fresh collection of power, he snaked out invisible tentacles of energy that he used to hold the aircraft afloat until all of the crew and passengers could be rescued by nearby commercial boats and FDNY marine vessels.

Providing additional buoyancy to the plane from such a distance proved to be a feat beyond anything Bryan had attempted before. But he managed to hold on for the fifteen minutes that it took to complete the full rescue.

Then, as his vision blurred and the pain surged, more intense than he had ever felt it, he collapsed to the deck of the ferry.

Everybody around him assumed he had fainted from witnessing the incident.

It wasn't until he woke up in the hospital a day later that Bryan learned he had had a massive stroke.

***

Somehow, the power he had been able to channel must have drained some portion of the natural tidal pools of his life energy. Of course that energy was limited. He must have always known; he'd just ignored it, been a slave to the driving obsession that he make a difference, that he be the hero.

That choice had left his body weak well before its natural time, and though he was merely in his mid-sixties, he looked like he was in his late seventies or even his early eighties.

Now he didn't have enough of his own life energy to reach his oxygen mask. And there was nobody close enough that he could draw life force from.

With his lungs burning from the lack of oxygen and dizziness beginning to lap at his mind, Bryan stared at the tipped canister of oxygen, at the thin line of transparent yellow tubing just out of reach.

Less than an inch from his trembling fingers, the oxygen hissed.

Teasing him, tantalizing him from just beyond his feeble reach.

The steady hiss mocked him.

Reminded him of another sound. The applause from an appreciative crowd gathered in the streets on the day White Vector had received the key to the city.

***

It was thirty years ago, just half a decade after he had made his first appearance at the Queensboro Bridge.

White Vector had established a pattern of daring rescues — assisting the fire department with saving people unable to navigate their way out of burning buildings, lifting debris to free people who had been pinned or trapped from collapsed construction sites, weather damaged buildings or vehicular accidents, and even providing emergency CPR. Channeling energy allowed Bryan to kick-start a failed heart without having to perform traditional compressions.

Surprisingly, there were very few confrontations with bad guys. Sure, he had thwarted the occasional mugger, robber, and even pickpocket, but most of the good White Vector had done had been akin to the work of New York's Bravest rather than the work of New York's Finest.

Bryan remembered the pride he had felt standing on the stage beside the mayor as the gray-haired gentleman presented a speech about him and a recent schoolhouse rescue by him and FDNY Rescue 1 two weeks previously; White Vector alone had been responsible for saving no less than one hundred lives.

"And, asking nothing in return for his selfless acts, White Vector worked diligently along the brave men and women of Rescue Company 1, repeatedly ignoring the danger and running back into the burning school to retrieve every single person trapped inside.

"This most recent act is, of course, just one of many times that White Vector has stepped forth as a hero to the fine citizens of our glorious city. Which is why I am not only presenting him with the key to our city, but am also instituting him as an honorary member of New York City Fire Department Rescue Company 1."

The crowd responded with a thunderous burst of applause.

***

As the echoes of old applause rang through his head, Bryan's mind continued the dizzying spin, whirling, descending, into a sea of darkness.

His eyes, bloodshot and unfocused, tried desperately to target onto the oxygen line that eluded him and he hacked out choking breaths.

The most difficult thing Bryan had ever done had been to stay alone and single, to purposely avoid getting close to anybody, either as a friend or as a lover. It was a conscious decision made to protect others, keep them distant and safe from his vigilante life.

So he had consciously decided to live the course of his life alone.

No love.

No family.

No legacy to speak of.

The ultimate price of his secret identity, his hidden life as a hero.

Despite the parades, the celebrations, the lines of kids seeking White Vector's autograph, the cheers and the applause and the notoriety, he realized that it would all end alone.

Simply because, as a feeble old man with barely any strength any super ability left, his oxygen line had popped off and he was unable to reach it.

It was too humiliating.

Bryan had, of course, just in the past few years, known humiliation.

Public humiliation.

***

His ability to save the day had been significantly lessened ever since the stroke he had had that morning on the Staten Island Ferry.

With a weakened left side, Bryan had to concentrate hard

just to try to walk in a normal fashion when he was visible to the public, and his heroic acts were more akin to rescuing kittens or kites from trees than anything worthy of a comic book script plot. His main gig was giving inspirational talks at local public schools denouncing bullying.

So when he arrived at the scene of a bank hostage situation, and Officer Mahoney explained that there were three gunmen and five hostages, his first thought was wondering whether or not he should just leave it to the police. They had, after all, been doing just fine before he arrived.

But when the officer in charge, the one with the bullhorn, informed the bandits inside that White Vector was now here, that burst of pride took over.

Bryan stepped past the barricades of police cruisers and walked right up to the bank. He channeled the energy of the surrounding police officers, cognizant of how much additional effort just pulling energy in required, and used the energy to heighten his senses.

Halfway to the bank building, he could hear two of the robbers talking, panicked that he was approaching them so calmly and was able to determine their approximate location behind the walls and through the bright reflective glass of the bank.

This type of sensory enhancement typically helped him in combat because it made him more sensitive to picking up subtle changes in a person's chemistry and heartbeat before they acted; it gave him the split second of additional time he needed to have the upper hand in any sort of hand-to-hand combat.

Only, this time, while he was able to easily syphon energy to enhance his senses, his agility was still that of a recovered stroke victim.

So when he entered the door and the gunman to his far right fired, he wasn't able to dodge out of the way. And his reflexes were so slow that sending a blast of energy into the air to deflect the bullet just inches after it left the chamber didn't happen. The bullet made it all the way to Bryan, his late-acting energy bolt barely slowing the bullet as it punched into his right arm.

He had slowed the bullet down enough so that it didn't break his skin; but it still hit him hard like a good solid punch in the arm — something that, thirty years ago, he could have shrugged off the way one might shrug off a mosquito.

This one, though, hurt tremendously, putting him off guard.

What had he been thinking just walking straight into the building?

Sure, years ago, before the stroke, he could have easily sent energy bursts to disarm as many as half a dozen gunmen, then used his temporarily enhanced senses and increased strength to subdue the bad guys.

But that had been before.

Now, Bryan questioned what he was doing.

That's when the second gunman, the one directly in front of Bryan, fired.

He hadn't fired at Bryan, though. He shot one of the hostages. An older woman. One of the tellers. The bullet went into the back of her head and exited her face in a sickening explosion of blood, skin, and bone.

"I told you we weren't fooling around here!" the gunman shouted as the woman collapsed forward onto the cold tile floor.

The other hostages screamed, and another gunman, the one on Bryan's left, fired. His bullet struck a second victim, a middle-aged man in a gray suit, in the stomach. That man bowed over, clutching at his mid-section, and crumpled to his knees.

Bryan rushed at the gunman directly in front of him, channeling his rage and energy into his right arm. He batted the man's gun away just as he was attempting to fire another round at Bryan. The shot went wild and ricocheted off the ceiling. Bryan drove his fist into the man's face, knocking him out with a single blow.

He paused to pull in a short burst of energy from the man he had just felled before turning to his right and looking at the first gunman, the one who had fired at him when he entered. That gunman aimed at Bryan. This time, Bryan was ready for the shot and pushed a burst of energy straight at the bullet.

But instead of stopping the bullet, the energy deflected it into the neck of an older gentleman who had been sitting up against the wall.

Bryan rushed at the shooter, slapped his gun-hand away, and elbowed him in the gut. As the man fell, Bryan sent a mental airshove, launching the man across the lobby where he struck his head hard against a marble pillar.

The third gunman seized that opportunity to rush out the front door.

And that's where, immediately outside the front door, he was apprehended by New York's Finest.

Three of the five hostages had been shot.

Because Bryan had been too feeble to properly handle the situation.

Bryan took in a deep breath, felt the trembling in his bones, the throbbing in his head from the energy it had taken. His upper lip was matted with blood from the burst vessels in his nose.

But there was another damp and sticky part of his body. He had lost control of his bowels.

Not the best thing to happen when you were wearing a mostly white costume.

***

Like in that humiliating moment in the bank, the one that had ended his career, Bryan felt his bowels let go again.

And, as the lack of oxygen made him feel as if every single nerve was being torn apart, the ripples of the surrounding darkness started to intrude.

Just as he began to let go, a clean and cool burst of oxygen filled Bryan's lungs.

He hacked and choked, feeling the sweet breath that filled his airways.

At that point he realized that someone was standing over him; the someone who had moved the oxygen mask back onto Bryan.

Bryan slowly opened his eyes, the light a stabbing pain, but could make out the shape of a young man with short dark hair standing before him.

"Mr. Rand," the young man said. "Can you hear me?"

"Y—yeah," Bryan breathed out, his throat still sore and raw. "Yes."

"You're going to be okay."

The man grabbed Bryan by the wrist, pressing his fingers into the underside of it. "I'm just going to check your pulse, Mr. Rand."

"Who . . . are . . . you?" Bryan said.

"I'm the new nurse that has been assigned to this ward. I'll be taking care of you now, Mr. Rand. My name is Robert."

As Brian's vision came into focus he could make out the sharp jaw line and ruggedly handsome features of the young man, likely in his early thirties. Bryan looked down from the young man's face to the gold pocket watch he held in his hand, using it to keep time of Bryan's pulse.

"Robert?"

"Yes."

"Nobody . . . uses a . . . pocket watch . . . any . . . more."

"This was my grandfather's watch, sir." Robert said. "He received it when he retired from the fire department. He passed it along to me when he died."

"Fire . . . fighting," Bryan gasped, "is a good calling."

"Yes," Robert said. "And it's something I've wanted to do as long as I can remember. I was in a car accident when I was quite young. I don't remember it, but my Mom liked to tell me the story of how White Vector saved me. I wanted to be like him, and like my granddad, too. Only my asthma means I failed the physical three times. So I became a nurse." He shrugged. "At least I can still make a difference."

His vision much clearer, Bryan looked up at the blue-green of the young man's eyes and recognized a conviction he hadn't seen since he was Robert's age and stood staring in a mirror.

He also recognized the tingling he'd first felt when he discovered his power. Something in the young man pulled at the remaining power left in Bryan's body.

As his foggy mind became clearer with each fresh breath of oxygen into his lungs, Bryan knew.

It was not over.

Succumbing to the gentle pull, Bryan pushed the mystical power that had coursed through his body in the young man's direction. The world-weight that he had carried on his shoulders started to let go as he could feel Bobby's body accepted the gift naturally, but his confused eyes told Bryan that he didn't seem to understand what was happening.

That's okay. He soon will.

"Bobby," Bryan whispered.

"Yes, Mr. Rand."

"I want you . . . to have something, son."

"What's that, sir?"

"The top drawer . . . of my . . . nightstand. Open it. There's a . . . brown leather box inside."

Robert moved over, opened the drawer, and looked inside.

"Take it out. Open it."

Robert did as requested.

While he did so, Bryan thought back to the day he had packed that leather box.

***

Bryan's companions at the NYPD had honored him by not mentioning the condition they'd found him in, Mahoney covered him in an EMT blanket so that nobody except the first few cops into the building had seen what he'd done to himself.

And, since not every hostage situation always worked out perfectly, there was no blatant blaming or accusing White Vector of any wrongdoing. With the exception, of course, of a few city reporters who had never been on the side of vigilante justice and used the incident as an excuse to further their position.

But Bryan knew better.

He knew that he could not be counted on to be the people's hero any longer.

He was a danger.

Weeks later, with trembling hands, he carefully folded the freshly laundered suit and tucked it into the box. Burning tears fell from his eyes and onto the white silk as he placed the key to the city on top of it.

Though he was firm in his resolve, he hadn't realized how difficult it would be to know he would never again put the costume on, never again come to anybody's rescue.

He shut the box, and the most significant part of his life with it.

***

Robert's eyes lit up as he opened the box.

"This," Robert said, "looks like the key to the city. And this white top, and red mask. It . . . it was *you.*" He looked up from the brown leather box and down at Bryan. "You're the one who saved me that day."

"I was," Bryan said. "Once. That costume, that key belonged . . . to White Vector . . . to me. But . . . I'm no longer him . . . I'm giving it to you."

Bryan knew that his days were numbered, that there would not be many more sunrises before him. But the young man who stood before him was his sign that it didn't have to end with him.

Bryan would teach Robert everything he knew. White Vector, the hero that the world needed, the people's hero, would live another day, in the eyes, heart, and mind of the young man who stood over him.

The sun would rise once more.

Collateral Damage

1

"I'm not a scavenger," Peter mumbled as he rifled through the jacket pockets of the dead man who lay crumpled against the alley wall. "I'm a sin-eater."

He had to keep telling himself this.

After all, scavengers feed on the dead. Peter fed on the living, was the force that took those lives. With each victim he could feel their life-force draining from them and channelling through his entire being, kick-starting orgasmic ripples of uncontrollable laughter that shot up and out from some dark core.

Peter was the harbinger of death.

He had been for years; and though he had suspected he was to blame for so very many deaths – his mother, during childbirth, his father just a few years later, his very first best friend, Donnie, then a dozen more friends, colleagues and teachers at school – it had just been in the past six months that it had become undeniable.

His stare killed people – it sucked the life-force right out of them.

He had spent several frustrated years trying to deny it and wailing in the pain of being at the centre of so much loss and tragic death; loved ones whose lives were cut short simply for their proximity to Peter O'Mallick.

He had tried to put an end to it.

Several times.

But for some reason, perhaps a side-effect of the curse that coursed through his veins, every single suicide attempt had proven fruitless; simply, he could not die by his own hand.

It was only recently that Peter realized this power, this inexplicable curse he had been born with, could be put to good use.

In an alley, one not unlike the one he was in now, he had accidentally killed a man; watched the side of his head explode when making eye contact with him. But, while standing over the dead body, again frustrated with his curse, he had discovered the man he had just killed had himself been a killer.

That changed everything.

It meant, finally, after all those years of *suffering the slings and arrows of his outrageous fortune*, Peter could *attempt to take arms against his sea of troubles*, apply his curse to a good cause, and prove to Hamlet that it didn't have to always be end in tragedy.

If he was cursed with causing death, the very least he could do was focus his time and energy on ridding the world of the low-lives, the carrion who fed off of the havoc, pain and loss of others.

That moment, the Peter O'Mallick who had railed against his curse took a back-seat to the new Peter who had embraced the power flowing within him as a force of good.

He had become a vigilante.

Stalking the dark alleys of Toronto, he had been able to pick away a living, living on the streets, avoiding crowds, homeless shelters or interacting much with others. He had seemed to have a natural instinct for finding the low-lives who fed off of society, sought to harm, hurt, steal and kill. And those were the people he unleashed his power on.

People like the dead man whose jacket pockets Peter was digging through. This man was part of a gang who had been threatening local shopkeepers with a "protection racket" by extorting cash from several businesses on Gerrard Street near Church.

It was funny how most people – not even low-lives like this extortionist – didn't pay any attention to the homeless when going about their business. Peter had been lying low, spending time in this particular neighbourhood as part of his regular roaming, never staying in one area for too long, particularly not after making a kill, when he had picked up on the man's activities.

He had watched this man, a stocky man with a red beard, and his partner, a lean, tall bald man who wore over-sized CHIPS-style reflection sunglasses, make their way through the neighbourhood shops, spending just a few minutes going inside each one.

Peter had lived long enough on the streets to understand they were up to something more than wanting to visit each shop – particularly when they returned each day.

After spotting them making their way through the exact same routine for the third day in a row, Peter planted himself inside the small pita shop, using pocket change to buy a bottle of water and then sit at one of the round tables and wait for one of them to make his way inside.

The shop owner greeted the red-bearded thug with a nervous smile, made him a shawarma unasked which was handed over without the exchange of money and said: "I pay, I pay. You keep me safe. Thank you," nodding nervously the whole time.

The extortionist glanced over at Peter, who was dressed in filthy, ragged clothes, and immediately dismissed him as a derelict and no threat to his business.

"That's right, Paco," the thug had said. "You pay, and you stay safe for another day."

At that point, Paco wiped his hands on his apron, popped the cash drawer open and handed the man a couple of green bills.

"Good boy, Paco," the bearded man said, sinking his teeth into his shawarma. Then, with a mouthful, mumbled, "See you again tomorrow."

Peter followed Red-beard out the pita shop, up Mutual Street and down an alley behind an auto service store. He waited for the man to come back out after doing his business there when he confronted him.

"Excuse me," Peter said to him when red-beard came back out of the rear staff entrance to the auto service bay, licking sauce and meat juices from his fingers. "May I have a word with you?"

"Fuck off," red-beard said with a dismissive wave, barely even looking at him. "Go and bum change off of someone else."

"That's not what I want," Peter said, taking a few steps closer.

The man kept walking toward Peter, shaking his head and reaching down to move his jacket aside, revealing the gun handle sticking out of the left side of his pants.

"I said 'Fuck off!'" the man said, now just a couple of feet in front of Peter and looking right at him. "Fuck off and die, or I'll pop a round in between your filthy eyes."

"I'll fuck off," Peter said, standing his ground as the man finally made solid eye contact with him. "But you're the one who's going to die."

Peter stared back at the man and felt the power of the death stare channeling through him and right into the man's being.

Red-beard's eyes widened in a sudden realization of terror and the hand poised over the handle of the gun suddenly clenched into a fist, as if the man was being seized by some sort of electric shock.

His left hand clutched at his chest as he fell to his knees, then dropped to the ground, his face making a loud smack as it connected with the pavement.

The uncontrollable reflexive laughter that came with each death bubbled up through Peter's throat and he released it like some satisfying post-death consumption burp.

A full-on shiver ran through Peter's body as the laughter ended, and he sunk down on one knee over red-beard's dead body.

As Peter crouched and rolled the man over, digging through his pockets, he reminded himself that he wasn't a scavenger.

He was a vigilante.

He was ridding the streets of the scum of society, cleansing the world of those who sought to hurt, to maim, to kill.

And in order to survive, he needed money. So he took it from the bad guys he put out of commission.

The way a carrion eater picked the flesh off the rotting bones of a dead animal carcass.

He shook his head, waving the thought away, and repeated the mantra to himself.

"I'm not a scavenger, I'm a sin-eater."

He still only partially believed it.

2

MICHAEL PACED BACK and forth in the tight space backstage, feeling the familiar rush of adrenaline with knowing that, in just a few minutes, he would be out there and at the mercy of the crowd.

His palms were slick, and his heart was racing; just enough to get him in the proper groove for a stand-up routine. He hadn't been to Toronto in years and wanted to ensure he knocked off a few jokes specific to Canada and to this city.

Local crowds always liked when you could do that.

He bounced a few times on the balls of his feet, feeling his heart rate get to the perfect state he needed it to be in before going on stage. It was all part of the routine, part of the set-up.

Michael had always loved comedy, particularly improv, and though he worked a full-time job he had pursued his passion with almost every free moment.

Jokes, one-liners and amusing observations came to him constantly, typically while he went about his every-day tasks. He had long been making note of them to use in his stand-up routine, had even sold some of his jokes to both Carson and Leno back in the day.

But he lived for the thrill and fun of being on stage, working the crowd, holding them in the palm of his hand. Continuing to pace, he waited for the host to introduce him, glancing at his watch one more time. The previous comic had gone over-time by a few minutes, and the host, who had already been operating in a deficit, went well over the five-minute segue. That put the whole evening close to 10 minutes behind. Michael had to take a deep breath and not let that get the better of him.

He reminded himself to focus on the crowd on the other side of those curtains, the jokes he would be telling, the wonderful moment of anticipation.

Finally, he heard the host finish off his bit and begin to introduce him.

"Ladies and gentlemen, all the way from Buffalo, New York, the one, the only, Michael C. Bass!"

The crowd applauded politely as the host went down the steps on the side of the stage and Michael stepped out from the break in the curtains.

"Good evening!" Michael said, trying to make out faces in the crowd under the harsh glare of the lights. It always took about a minute or so for his eyes to adjust, and he liked to pick a few people from the front row to gauge how he was doing.

He opened with a line that typically worked on winning over a Toronto audience.

"It's great to be back in Toronto: Tee-Oh, The Big Smoke, Hogtown, Little York, Hollywood North – or, as I like to call it, home of the CN Tower, North America's tallest erection."

The crowd tittered satisfactorily, so he moved on.

"Seriously, you've got to love a city that constantly inflicts penis envy on all of its neighbors."

More laughter.

"I've only gone up in the CN Tower once. That was enough for me. I'm not a big fan of heights. I never have been. I think it stems back to my first trip to Disney when I went on the Space Mountain ride. My daughter, who knew of my aversion to heights, warned me about it, but I didn't listen to her. I'm not sure if you're familiar with the Space Mountain roller coaster at Disney, but it's mostly in the dark; so I figured, if I couldn't see the height, it'd be okay.

"When the EMS team had to revive me at the end of the ride . . ." he paused to let the laughing subside, ". . . my daughter was standing there shaking her head. I also heard her mutter to the stranger beside her. 'Gee, Daddy, what's wrong with that man?'"

He paused, again, to let the audience digest that one, waited for the laughter to settle down, then continued.

"I've always been afraid of heights. Seriously, the 70's were terrifying for me, with all those platform and elevator shoes. Aw, heck, who am I kidding? There wasn't much about the 70's that I liked.

"Okay, there was one thing I liked about the 70's. The Paul Newman movie *Slapshot*. Are there any hockey fans in the crowd tonight?"

The crowd hooted and hollered.

"I love hockey. I think that's why I love Canada so much. Canada is serious about its hockey. Am I right?"

The crowd shouted their agreement.

"I've been a serious hockey fan my entire life. For me, it's a big deal. I go all out, wear a full suit and tie to each and every game I go to. And if I can't make it to a game, I'll sit there in my living room dressed to the nines. For effect, I even have a few friends over to cram beside me on the couch, thrust giant foam fingers in front of the TV to block my view, and spill beer and popcorn all over me.

"Being from Buffalo, I'm a Sabres fan," he paused for the expected boos and a few odd cheers. "But when I'm not cheering for my home team, I'm rooting for the Toronto Maple Leafs." *More cheering from the crowd, as expected.*

"I love the Toronto team. About the only thing that bothers me about these guys is the name. The proper plural term is "Leaves" not "Leafs" – but that's okay, they can get away with it, because of how many Stanley Cups the team has won in the past 40 years. No, wait, nix that. Well, at least the team has a snazzy blue and white uniform.

"What is it with fan loyalty to a team that hasn't won the cup since 1967? That's die-hard fandom and you've got to love that commitment. I think it's one of the reasons I love Maple Leaf fans: there's a sense of pride in working your ass off, putting your shoulder to the wheel and keeping at it, despite the odds."

The crowd cheered loudly at the compliment, and Michael basked in the rhythm he had fallen into.

There was something satisfying about manipulating a crowd, a deeply personal sense of accomplishment to bring mirth to complete strangers.

Unbeknownst to Michael, one particular member of his audience was laughing out of joy at his jokes rather than as the uncontrollable reflex to taking someone's life.

3

THE SOUND COMING out of Peter's throat had felt foreign and odd, but also strangely comforting.

It was pure, simple, mirth-inspired laughter.

When was the last time he had done that?

This Bass character was good. And a wonderful diversion from the mission that had brought Peter into the comedy club this evening.

Peter had followed the lean tall bald man here, having lost him for several hours after dealing with red-beard. It wasn't until the early evening that Peter had spotted him again.

Before Peter had been able to get the man alone, Baldy had slipped in to this comedy club.

Rather than wait outside, Peter figured he would head in, try to get a bite to eat and make the best of his wait.

Tucked away in the furthest corner of the crowded club, determined to avoid making eye contact with anybody, Peter focused on his mark while wolfing down a greasy burger and fries.

Baldy sat right up front, laughing loudly at every quip.

It wasn't until this Bass guy got on stage that Peter felt himself beginning to actually enjoy the comedy on stage.

There was something about him that Peter liked.

He imagined this Bass fellow would be a fun-loving friend.

It was an interesting fantasy, but the thought reminded Peter of just how long it had been since he had had a friend.

All of his own friends were either dead or far enough away from Peter to now be safe; at least to the best of his knowledge.

Because the deaths that Peter caused hadn't all been instantaneous; some of them had taken longer to manifest.

Like the cancer eating away at Sarah's father.

Sarah.

Peter felt a sharp stab of pain when thinking about her, about the tender moments they had together, about the long-ago dreams they'd shared about their common future, about the talks late into the night while they held each other and swore they would always be there for one another, about making love to Sarah while looking her deep in the eyes.

That was the clincher.

Sarah was missing and presumed dead. She was last seen here in Toronto, mixed up in some sort of drug-related activity; at least that's what it looked like, based on the fact that she was last seen with her cousin, whose body was found abandoned in a downtown alley, dead from a drug overdose.

That was originally what Peter had been doing here. Living on the streets, looking for any sign of Sarah, but also working his way through the darker part of society and attempting to use his death curse to make a positive difference.

He had to, after all, make up for all of those innocent people his curse had taken over the years.

So many deaths. So many loved ones; so many friends.

Peter rejected the thought of becoming friends with this Michael C. Bass.

It simply wouldn't be a good thing. Not if this Bass fellow wanted to stay alive.

Nobody who Peter cared about seemed to survive becoming close to him.

Which further highlighted Peter's dilemma. He needed to find Sarah, to know that she was alive, to ensure she was okay. But he couldn't get close to her again for fear that the growing curse ripening inside him would kill her.

The thought that Sarah was still out there, still alive, was the one thing that kept Peter going, kept him focused, and able to deal with the memories of so many deaths.

Peter's train of thought was broken when he spotted Baldy getting up.

Was he leaving the club?

Baldy headed off to the restrooms, so Peter relaxed again for a moment, deciding to pick at the fries on his plate and finish them off. If Baldy left, after all, Peter would follow him. And it was best to eat this rare meal while he could.

He focused his mind back on the stage.

The comedian was riffing on a new topic now.

"I'm honest to a fault," Bass said. "And it doesn't really win me many friends.

"When a woman asks if a dress makes her look fat, I give her the God's honest truth. 'Like a hippo,' I say. Of course, I'm simply honest, but not mean. If I were mean I'd go on to say. 'It's not really the dress, honey. It's your gigantic ass. That's what the real problem is here. The dress is fine. It's your huge ass that makes the dress look fat.'

"But I don't go that far. I'm honest, not cruel.

"My friends have often wondered what the *C* in my name stands for. I tell them 'Collateral' – as in 'Collateral Damage.'

"I can't keep my honesty in check, particularly when there's a joke to be had. So sometimes, in pursuit of a laugh, that next funny one-liner, there are unintended victims. Collateral.

"But humor is good. Laughter brings goodness to the world. And honesty is good, too. So making humor out of honesty, bringing a little more good to the world, makes that little bit of collateral damage acceptable."

4

PETER WAS FOLLOWING the comedian's latest chain of dialogue so closely that he almost didn't notice Baldy's exit. But he did manage to spot him out of the corner of his eye and tracked his movement. Baldy had moved from the hallway that led to the bathroom and ducked along the corridor that appeared to lead backstage.

Peter considered his unfinished fries, aware of how rare it was that he had a square meal. But he couldn't stay to finish them – he had to keep on the bald man's trail.

He got up, made his way across the bar and headed toward the corridor Baldy had taken. When he got to the end, there was a left turn that led to the back-stage area and a right turn which led to a series of doors, likely the office, a couple of dressing rooms and perhaps a green room. All of the doors were closed.

Peter decided to turn left.

He took only a few steps, could still hear the comedian, Bass, performing his routine on the other side of the curtains, but he also heard something else.

A hollow dragging noise.

He stopped to listen.

Something was being dragged across the floor. And it was coming from the dark shadows on Peter's right, just around the corner from where he stood.

He waited a moment, hoping his eyes would adjust to the light, then stepped forward and peeked around the corner.

Baldy was turned away from Peter and dragging a large topless cardboard box back away from the corner. The three-foot-high box, a couple of feet across and wide, was filled to capacity with what looked like stage props, signs, lighting fixture supplies and other occasionally used stage and backstage objects.

When Baldy finished dragging this box out, he moved around it to push a larger wooden crate along the wall.

What the hell was he up to?

Peter's curiosity got the better of him, and, instead of making his move, he kept watching.

Baldy finished shoving the crate aside, he knelt down in front of a vent in the wall, pulled something out of his back pocket, what appeared to be a jackknife, and used either the blade or a flathead screwdriver attachment to pry the metal vent grate out from the wall.

Then he reached inside and pulled something out.

It appeared to be a handgun.

Shit.

Peter realized he only had a moment to surprise Baldy without the risk of being shot, and was about to step fully around the corner when a loud and familiar voice from behind startled him.

"Hey, Bub, what's going on?"

Peter turned and saw Michael Bass, the comedian, standing a few feet behind him, a bemused look on his face. He must have finished his on-stage act and was heading back toward the greenroom.

"Shit!" Peter said, about to warn the comedian to get the hell out of there.

Still on from the stage, or perhaps because he was always "on" Michael replied. "Shit? If that's what you're looking for, you've taken a wrong turn, my friend. The men's room is just back thataways."

"No," Baldy said stepping up between them, the gun trained on them. "You've both taken a wrong turn."

"What the hell?" Michael said, automatically thrusting his hands up in the air.

Baldy positioned himself a few feet away, the gun in his left hand slowly sweeping back and forth between Peter and Michael.

Peter stared at Baldy, squinting hard, trying to get the man to look into his eyes. But it didn't seem to be working. Either it was too dark, and the man couldn't see his eyes, or Baldy was distracted, his eyes flitting quickly between Peter and Michael. Perhaps it was a combination of both, but Peter's curse, his power, didn't seem to be working. He figured he needed to get Baldy into a lighted area.

"Hand over your wallets and you won't get hurt," Baldy said.

"You don't want to do that," Michael said. "All I have is US money, and with the exchange rates the way they are you're not really going to get a good value. Might I suggest-"

But Baldy cut him off by reaching out and smacking him on the side of the head. "Knock it off! I said hand over your fucking wallet."

Peter used that distraction to move.

Not being a person of action – his idea of sports was playing interactive video games on the Wii or Xbox 360 Kinect – Peter had never really been in a fight before. But having been a child of the television era, having watched hundreds of action movies, in particular, the entire Karate Kid series as well as virtually every single superhero flick ever made, he seemed to know somewhat what he could do to quickly disarm Baldy.

Or so he thought.

He took a few steps forward, successfully knocking Baldy's gun hand to the side with an outward swing of his right arm and charging into the man's chest with his left shoulder.

Baldy stumbled back, into a tall wooden backdrop, a bit off balance, but still on his feet.

The gun was still in his hand.

So much for my career as a superhero, taking out bad guys with a single attack, Peter thought.

Baldy regained his balance and trained the gun back on Peter.

"Enough bullshit," he said.

The sound of a couple of people talking echoed from the hallway that led to the greenrooms and the office.

"Shit!" Baldy said.

"As I mentioned, the men's room is-"

"Shut your pie-hole!" Baldy said, cuffing Michael in the head, then turning and running to the far side of the stage and running out a door with a bright exit sign.

"You okay?" Peter asked Michael, who nodded that he was. "Good. Stay here, get help. I'm going after him."

Peter then ran for the exit, pushed his way through the door which wasn't yet half-closed, and saw that it led to an exit, likely to the alley, and a set of stairs going up. His thought was that Baldy would have headed outside, but the door was closed, and, he noticed, had an emergency exit alarm bar on it.

So, Baldy hadn't gone out; he must have gone up.

Peter paused, listened and could hear the sound of footsteps echoing from up the stairwell.

Baldy was moving fast.

Peter hoofed it up, grabbing onto the handrail to pull himself around each corner.

The sound of Baldy's footsteps continued to echo through the stairwell, meaning he hadn't stopped at any of the levels on the way up. Despite being out of breath, Peter did his best to keep running.

Baldy was faster than Peter, and by the time Peter had ascended what seemed at least a dozen floors, he had to pause and catch his breath. The sound of Baldy running hadn't abated, so Peter pushed himself to keep moving forward, despite the knife of pain in his side and his own loud panting sound echoing through the stairwell.

A few minutes later the sound of running footsteps coming from above stopped, followed mere seconds later by a loud thud and CRACK.

He tried to put on a bit more speed.

When he finally reached the top of the stairwell, and stood, breathless, beside the door at the top, he noticed the broken padlocked latch, figuring it was likely an entrance to the roof.

Peter estimated they were about twenty stories up.

He slowly pushed the door all the way open.

Baldy wasn't anywhere within sight on the part of the roof Peter could see from the doorway.

He stepped out from the doorway, looking to his left and right, and, not seeing anything, wondered if Baldy had jumped to an adjacent rooftop.

The answer came quickly and without warning, in the form of a heavy body slamming into his lower back from above and behind. Peter stumbled forward a few steps then crumpled to the rooftop as the weight of a full-sized man pushed down on his upper back and shoulders.

As he fell, the blow of the gun handle striking him on the back of the head felt like it had meant to be a direct hit, but was likely reduced in intensity by the angle of the two falling men.

Lucky he had crumpled so quickly, Peter thought.

Then he was on his knees, Baldy still on top of him.

Peter rolled forward, hoping to toss Baldy overtop of himself.

It only partially worked. Baldy was still half on Peter's back, sending another punch. This time the man's naked right fist struck at the back of Peter's head; and this time it connected, sending a bright flash of pain through Peter's vision.

He let out a yell, buckled, and managed to knock Baldy most of the way off of his back. He kicked out, his foot connecting with Baldy's left shoulder. Baldy's gun clattered a few feet away on the rooftop.

Peter knew he only had a few seconds to get up, get the upper hand on Baldy. It might have been dark in the backstage area, but at least there was ambient light from the taller nearby building windows casting down onto the rooftop. Light enough for Baldy to be able to see Peter's eyes, to feel the wraith of his death curse.

Peter took a few steps back, closer to the edge of the building, closer to a part of the roof that would cast more light on him.

Baldy got up, and took a few steps backwards, pausing to reach for the gun. Then he turned and pointed it at Peter.

Their eyes met.

And that's when Michael appeared in the doorway, just a few feet away.

"I thought it over," Michael said, his hands already thrust into the air, as he stepped out of the doorway. "My US cash might not be worth that much, but you look like a smart fellow. I figure you'll put it away, hang onto it, watch the markets and exchange it for Canadian funds once the economy shifts back to normal."

Baldy turned, facing Michael, aiming the gun at him. Michael winked at Peter and smiled, their eyes meeting straight on for the first time, Peter getting a clear view of Michael's eyes, Michael having a clear view of Peter's.

No! Peter thought. But it was too late when the thought came into his mind.

"Fuck off with those stupid jokes," Baldy said, and pulled the trigger.

A loud explosion of gunfire shattered the night air and a small pimple of blood sprouted on Michael's chest. He looked down at it, a look of complete shock on his face.

"You . . . shot . . . me . . ." Michael said as if arousing from a deep sleep; then, his quick wit suddenly surfaced and he said. "And ruined a damn fine shirt, I might add."

At that, Michael stumbled forward, directly toward Baldy, his arms out, as if stepping forward to embrace the thug in a giant bear hug.

Baldy stood there watching Michael lumber forward and collapse right into his arms. The two shuffled backwards on the roof as if they were an ill-matched novice student and dance instructor awkwardly practicing a routine neither knew to the wrong music.

Then then took two more steps backward, right to the edge of the roof, and they both dropped off.

Peter ran to the edge, in time to see the two bodies slam in unison into the top of a garbage dumpster in the alley below.

Despite his breathlessness, the uncontrollable laughter bubbled up from the base of his stomach and filled the night air with an insane stream of cackling.

It lasted almost half a minute, and when the mad burst of laughter finally subsided, Peter took a few steps forward and peeked over the edge. He looked down at the street twenty-odd floors below at the two dead men, their bodies still intertwined like star-crossed lovers, and shook his head.

Sure, he took the bad guy down, but why did his curse also have to kill an innocent man?

It was a senseless waste of a good life.

But at least Baldy was taken out.

What was it that Bass had said when he'd been on stage?

Something about collateral damage. *That bringing a little more good to the world, makes that little bit of collateral damage acceptable.*

The world now had one less good guy, but also two less bad-guys.

Acceptable collateral for a day's work.

"I'm a sin-eater," Peter mumbled, walking away from the edge of the rooftop. "A harbinger of death."

The Zombie Whisperer

"Hey Chancie!" Stuart called out. "Bet you don't have the balls to French kiss that zombie."

"Yeah, LaChance. I double-dare you!" Bruce said. "Lay one on her!"

"I'll lay one on her once I see you lay your money down, boys," Robert LaChance said, getting up from the bar stool where the three of them had been gulping down McMenamins Rubinator beers.

You see, Robert LaChance would do almost anything to win a bet or prove his buddies wrong. Completion of either one came with the same smug satisfaction that fueled their competitive relationship.

It wasn't the money; it was the winning.

Winning a bet was everything.

Following through on an outrageous dare was what life was about.

And, lately, the bets, and the adrenaline rush had been happening between intervals that seemed far too long.

Over the years, Robert and two of his best pals backed each other into the must cocked-up precarious situations imaginable. It involved elements of posturing, name-calling and tens of thousands of dollars exchanged between the three of them. From jumping out of planes, off tall bridges and cliff faces to death-defying stunt driving on a mountainous costal highway to deep-sea diving in shark-infested waters, there was barely a stunt one could conceive of that the three of them hadn't added an extra layer of dangerous stupidity to and bet the other ones they wouldn't be able to pull it off.

The surprising thing about this ridiculous lifestyle, however, was how this immature thrill-seeking behaviour become a key that just might save humanity from this confusing and horrifying worldwide plague.

And to think it all started right here in this bar, not five months ago.

You look like you don't believe me.

Tell you what – grab yourself another drink and get one for me – I'll take a Mac's Amber – and I'll tell you the whole story.

You with me, junior?

Good. When you first sat down you looked like you could use a little escape from the grind; like you could loosen up a bit and unwind.

Make yourself comfortable, sport, because I think you're going to enjoy this little tale.

So, being a regular here now for the past twenty years, I got to know Robert, Stuart and Bruce pretty well, when they started coming in about eight years ago. They always came in every Wednesday night like clockwork and they always sat on those same three stools, just on that edge of the bar over there. Huey, Duey and Luey, I called them before I learned their names. They came in together, always on the same night and they always took up the exact same seats; and if those stools were occupied, they turned and duck-walked their asses out of the bar like a gaggle of upset old ladies whose favourite teller isn't working at the bank branch that day.

They drank adventure, they loved taking risks and they loved betting, laying down money on almost anything and everything they could.

But you change their weekly bar-visit routine, and look out Charlie – you'd have three pissy little sissies on your hand.

But I digress.

When not stuck in this local hangout routine, they craved risk; they thrived on it.

There is apparently an adrenaline rush that comes with laying it out on the line like that. I wouldn't know. I punch a clock, file the papers I need to, and then come back here and drink away my free time. That, and listening to the common gossip, and spreading a little bit of it to anyone whose ear I can bend, is enough for me.

In any case, sitting here, listening in on their conversations, and occasionally shooting the shit with them, I learned a lot about the three of them.

They all grew up on the same street not too far from here in a residential section in central Hillsboro. Robert and Stuart's parents owned houses right beside one another and Bruce's folks owned a house across the street. They were all born within eighteen months of each another.

Legend has it that when they were in diapers the three used to egg one another on from their strollers as their mothers pushed them around. And, depending on who you talk to, they actually got their mothers to walk faster, if not run, as if subconsciously pushed forward by the silent insistence of their three strong-willed children.

All three came from white upper middle-class families, their fathers employed by two of the largest *Silicon Forest* employers, the mothers all members of the Oregon PTA; and you can be sure all three families sat front and center in their Sunday best each weekend at the local mass.

Some might speculate that it was this cushy well-preserved and protected environment that set the three off. Me, I think the jury is still out on that one. All I know is that they started daring each other and making bets over the stupidest things from the earliest years.

In the winter months when a local creek froze, they would delight in walking across the thin ice, moving along the surface until they heard and felt the cracks beneath them. The last person to vacate the ice before it broke through was declared the winner. You'd lose, of course, if your foot went into the brown muddy water of the creek.

Back then they'd bet using comic books and bubble gum trading cards for collateral.

When they got a bit older, the risks increased, and so did the currency of their bets.

Do you remember the original lawn darts? Not the plastic ball-like tipped ones you can find now, but the originals. The heavy ones with the rounded metal tips?

They must have been no more than eight or nine when they would sneak far enough away across a field adjacent to Stuart's parents' house and play their very first game of lawn dart chicken.

Although they didn't call it *Lawn Dart Chicken*. They called it *Poleman Chicken Toss*.

That's where two of them would stand three feet apart from one another. They were called the Polemen. A dozen yards down the field stood the guy with all the darts. He was called the Tosser. The Tosser would pitch the darts as close to the Polemen as he could, and he would get a point for every time he got one within two feet of either of the Polemen (double points for getting one in the sweet spot between the two of them), and lose points every time he hit one of them.

The Polemen would lose a point if they moved or flinched at all while a dart was in the air, and gain a point for every time they stood their ground while being shot at.

The games were always really tight between the three, with regular tie games and in the early days, when their aim wasn't as good, with just as many bruises, scars and abrasions on virtually every body part as they acquired points.

The points translated into single dollars, which was about the right value to match the money they had available to them through their allowances.

When they discovered archery in the seventh grade, they concocted a new favourite game that they called *Airshot Roulette*. It was a lot simpler, but the states were much higher. One of them would take their bow and aim an arrow straight into the air, then the three of them would stand in one spot, watching the arrow disappear into the sky, often obscured in the blur of the sun, then tumble down to earth. The goal was for them to stay rooted in their spot while the arrow came down. The one standing closest to where the arrow landed without flinching won the game. And this time the winner got their homework done by the losers, usually equally divided.

After dozens of rounds of the game over the course of a couple of years, there were only two injuries, but endless hours of an amazing adrenaline surge, and lots of saved hours where the winner got to skip out on hours of laborious math equations or boring essay composition.

One time an arrow caught in the side of the left foot, tearing a hole into the side of his sneaker and punching through the rubber of his sole, leaving an ugly gouge in the side of his foot. And on another occasion, an arrow found a home in the top of Bruce's right shoulder and the tip came out the other side a few inches down his back on his right side.

As Bruce wailed in pain, the stories go that Robert cursed, since his pal had finally bested his record for closest blood-drawing arrow, and Stuart let out a high pitched laugh saying: "Dammit, Robert. Now we have to cut my lucky arrow."

"All I know," Bruce hissed out between screams of pain. "Is that you two bitches will be doing my homework for the rest of the fuckin' year!"

They managed to snip the tip of the arrow and withdraw the shaft from the wound and treat it. One thing the three had become was proficient at dressing wounds; Lord knows they had inflicted enough injuries on one another over the years. So they were able to dress Bruce's wound and keep the injury hidden from his parents. Fortunately, there was no devastating damage; but even today he has some limited movement when he tries to raise his right arm overhead – and he can't do the full 360-degree spin of his arm without letting out a gut-wrenching scream.

The stunts and the bets went on like that, you see, until the three of them went off to college. Then it cooled down a bit. At least for a few years, because they were all separated during that time.

But that indefeasible passion within each of them never left; and it showed in the professions they each chose.

Stuart became a logger, attracted by what has been deemed the most dangerous profession in America, and he now works as a Logging Supervisor for the Oregon Department of Forestry right here in Forest Grove. Bruce became a pilot and owns a charter company that flies out of Astoria. And Robert, or Chancie, as his buddies still call him, became a snake handler in Portland.

The professions they chose gave them some of the thrills that they thrived on; but it didn't give them the additional challenge of the dare and of the bets.

That's why the three ended up getting back in contact with one another – it's like there was something critical missing from their lives when they didn't have that special camaraderie. And they made sure to plan getaways where they could engage in risk taking behavior, laying bets on various aspects of the outcomes.

For most guys, all it took was heading off to a strip club or for a wild night on the town without the wives; but for these three, it was all about the death-defying thrills, all about placing bets and double-dares, and being in the ultimate death-defying situations.

So that's the kind of guys they were. And I know I spent a while telling you specifics about it, but I think it's important for you to know that, to understand the intensity of their risk rituals before I get back to explain what happened with the zombie.

It's funny when you think about zombies now, isn't it? There were always TV shows and movies and books that all speculated about what might happen if people came back from the dead as zombies.

But when it happened, nobody expected that it would be just another disease that we learned to live with. I mean, sure, you get infected, you eventually die, you come back and are obsessed with eating flesh. But there was no mass outbreak, no apocalyptic collapse of society.

The disease exists, it is transmitted through zombie bite, and for the most part, the rest of us survive, while an unfortunate few fall prey to the toxin we know as the *zombivirus*.

I mean, I've read countless articles and papers speculating on the origin of the disease; and they all conflict with one another. There are as many possible origin stories about this as there are about the creation of the pyramids. We'll never know, will we, junior? But the reality is, they exist, the disease continues to be spread, and there's no cure.

At least there wasn't a cure; until recently.

Because Robert LaChance, our boy Chancie, might have inadvertently discovered a cure for the *zombivirus* due to some smart ass bet from his pals. And imagine that; an antidote to the whole mess. Meaning, if you get bit by a zombie, your death isn't certain, we don't need to chop your head off and cremate you to prevent you from coming back.

There's a possibility, now, that you could be saved. You don't need to die and then come back in the undead state.

I mean, the virus has been around now a good five years. At least since the first documented case that gained media attention. And we know the virus is slowly getting worse, continuing to spread, ever so slowly.

We've done our best, of course, to move on, to live with the knowledge that the *zombivirus* exists. And we've done quite well. But, much like AIDS or HIV, it's still there, and continues to slowly spread, no matter how much we bury our heads in the sand and try to just go on living.

Part of the problem might stem from the fact that, unlike the common pop culture stories about zombies, it could take up to three months before a zombie bite infection would actually kill you, turning you into a zombie. This slow effect, unlike the fictional immediate death, made the threat less concrete – almost like the threat of eventual lung cancer from smoking.

I mean, if smokers might randomly have their head explode the second they lit up a cigarette, avid smokers might quit cold turkey. But because the disease in a person's lungs takes years to manifest, the risk seems inherently abstract, and less of a pressing concern.

That's likely how the zombie epidemic ended up taking hold. The manifestation of an infection leading to death took at least a couple of months.

So people were infected without knowing it.

And people went on living their lives and the devastation of the zombivirus become a backdrop for everyday activities.

This bar, as you must know, as a good example.

Following a trend that has seemed to have spread throughout the United States, it has a zombie feed challenge. The spread of that as a popular bar activity has replaced the previous trend of mechanical bulls as a way to demonstrate a person's machismo.

Here at Hank's Bar & Grill, like so many other bars, we've got our own zombie feed challenge mascot. Have you met Simone? She's in the back room, just on the other side of the dance floor. And yes, she's chained in the same space that the mechanical bull used to stand before it broke down.

That damn bull sat there, broken and unattended to for years before they finally replaced it.

But the zombie feed challenge brought some life back into the concept of bar stunts, now didn't it?

At Hanks's we have three levels of zombie feed. There's the standard safe chunk of red meat. Feeding those to a zombie, provided you wear the rubber gloves, is relatively benign. The zombie is so drawn to the red, bloody hunk of meat that it doesn't even bother to try to grab the human holding it. It follows nature's mandate, and goes for the path of least resistance and the optimal choice.

Level two, which involves feeding the zombie a piece of pork rind is a bit more dangerous, since there isn't the immediate scent of the bloody hunk of steak to distract the zombie with, making it more likely the zombie will try to grab your arm and take a bite out of you. When you're feeding it a hunk of pork rind, you have to be a lot more nimble in order to feed it without it grabbing at you, since you smell as tasty to it as the pork rind itself.

And the third level, the highest challenge, is feeding Simone a piece of dog kibble. Because of the small size of the hunk of dried food, and the underwhelming scent of it, few people try that level of the challenge.

But it has become a popular activity. And sure, there have been the occasional reported casualty from the sport, but pictures of people taking the zombie feed challenge are all over the internet, posted on virtual every social media site. The number of people who have tried the level one challenge, and gotten a picture of themselves feeding the bar zombie has grown tremendously in the past year. If you were brave enough to try karaoke back in the day, then you likely tried the level one zombie feed challenge. That, at least, is the same in most bars. And a lot of them, unlike Hank's, don't have a level two or level three.

So how about you, junior? Have you done the level one challenge?

No?

You haven't even tried level one? A strapping young thing like you? I have to admit I'm a bit surprised.

Well, don't worry, champ, neither have I. I'm happy to hear the tales and share them with others; but I'm not all that interested in getting that close and personal with a freakin' zombie. It's bad enough I've got to share this planet with them, thank you very much.

So, in any case, Hank's here has had the zombie feed challenge, and you can be as sure as shit that Robert, Bruce and Stuart all tried the level three challenge, even without gloves, almost immediately.

The act was simply too tame for the three.

But they were sitting there, at the end of the bar, reminiscing about some of the grand adventures they had been on, some of the incredible dares and bets they had taken, and starting to feel sorry for themselves.

It seemed like, because they were getting older, they were settling down, taking less risks; and yes, I mean less risks outside each of their chosen professions.

But the three of them were getting visibly maudlin as they sat there at the bar. Their creative juices, the things that used to drive them to challenge one another, to bet and dare one another, seemed to have started to wither away.

I felt sad for them, actually.

But then, after a hot young college student walked in, catching the stray eyes of the three young men as they each, simultaneously eyed the tight little ass of her black designer jeans, Robert piped up.

"I dare you to go grab that ass," he said, poking Stuart in the ribs. "I've got fifty bucks says you won't. Walk up to her, don't say a single thing and grab a nice mitt-full of that luscious ass."

"Fuck that," Stuart replied. "I'll double the stakes and dare you to introduce yourself as the local breast inspector and grab both of her tits. I bet you another fifty that she'll kick you in the balls within the first second you lay a hand on her."

"No," Bruce said. "I dare either of you to grab an ass cheek in one hand, a tit in the other, and lean in and kiss her, sticking your tongue down her throat."

The three of them laughed.

"Hell," Robert said. "What are we doing? Where's the risk in that? Sure, she'll kick you in the nuts, slap your face, punch you in the stomach, and maybe call the cops. What's the risk? Where's the danger?"

"She could bite your tongue," Bruce said.

"Big deal," Robert said. "It's a little pain, a little blood. It's not like Simon back there biting your tongue." Robert was, of course, referring to Simon, our resident zombie.

"That's it!" Stuart said.

"What is?" Robert asked.

Stuart started laughing so hard that he doubled over and almost fell off his stool.

"Oh man, I've got a good one," he said, when he regained his composure.

"What?" Robert asked again.

"Hey Chancie!" Stuart called out, "Bet you don't have the balls to French kiss that zombie!"

"Yeah, LaChance." Bruce said. "I double-dare you! Lay one on her!"

"I'll lay one on her once I see you lay your money down, boys," Robert LaChance said, getting up from the bar stool where the three of them had been gulping down McMenamins Rubinator beers.

Have you tried the Rubinator beer? It's good. I see you're almost done your drink already. You should order one. You have to ask for them to mix a Ruby Ale with a Terminator Stout. It's not on the menu; it's something you have to know to ask about.

So anyways, Robert gets up, waits for his pals to each lay a series of hundred-dollar bills on the bar, and then pulls out one of the oldest barbs the three often liked to trade with one another.

"Kissing Simone is going to remind me of what it was like to kiss your mother, Brucie."

"Hey, fuck you, Chancie!"

They moved away from the bar to the back room, and me and half of the people around the bar followed them. The slowly building crowd also created a barrier between Robert and the bar staff, who would have tried to prevent the stupid stunt from taking place. I mean, it was one thing to do the zombie feed challenge. But to get that up close and personal, not following the protocol that was outlined, that was stepping beyond the bounds.

It had been at least a couple of days since Simone had been fed. So she was pretty animated and desperate. Not that it was easy to figure out the levels of desperation in a zombie. I mean I've only ever seen a handful of them in my time, and Simone is the one I've seen most often – she's been at Hank's here for a good eight months – but they all pretty much always act desperate and hungry all the time. Except, maybe, in that initial moment when they are tearing into the meat they've been fed.

In any case, Simone was animated and lunging at the end of the very short two feet of ankle bracelet chain she was allotted in the space she occupied.

As Robert approached, her arms were flailing out in front of her, reaching desperately to try to pull the succulent human flesh presented so close to her in.

"Ready for this?" Robert said, stepping to within a half inch just outside of Simone's reach.

"Go for it!" Stuart replied.

Robert darted in, quick as a fox, and with both of his hands he managed to grab Simone's wrists and hold her arms down at her sides. Then he deftly stepped in as he pulled her against him. It threw her off balance from her attempt to lunge forward, and she collapsed against him, her chest pressing up against his.

That's when Robert leaned in, turning his head slightly sideways, and darted his head down, pressing his lips against her open mouth.

Bruce and Stuart led the crowd in loud woops and hollers.

A split second passed before an odd groan came from Robert's throat and he pulled back, tearing his face from hers, pushing the zombie away, a fine spray of blood issuing from his mouth as he pulled back.

"She bit my fucking tongue!" Robert yelled, stumbling back, hand to his mouth. "She tore the tip of my tongue right off!"

"Oh, Jesus!" Stuart said. "I didn't think you'd do it, man. What the hell?"

"Oh, Chancie," Bruce said. "You're fuckin' toast man. She bit you. You're fuckin' toast."

Robert continued to stumble back, a look of sheer terror in his eyes. I'd never seen any of the three of them look scared before; but the look in this guy's eyes went well beyond fear. He was mortified.

He didn't say anything for a full minute.

The crowd, gasping and oohing and ahhing, didn't say anything while he stood there.

"Fuck this!" Robert suddenly said, walking back to the bar, reaching over, and taking a shot glass from behind it. "I've got a few months before I kick it, and I'll be damned if I'm going to let one fucking zombie bite stop me."

"What are you going to do, Chancie?" Stuart said.

"I'm going to do something I do every day with the fuckin' snakes. I'm going to milk Simone for her venom, and I'm going to create an antidote."

"How the fuck is that possible?" Bruce said.

"I'm a goddamn snake handler. Trust me. I know a thing or two about how this works for snakes. So why won't it work for the zombie venom?"

And he did just that. He went back into the ring with Simone, held her down, less afraid of being scratched or bitten, since he was already infected, and he collected her saliva into the shot glass.

He crammed the glass into her mouth and milked saliva out of her in much the same manner that he milked venom from rattlers and brown snakes.

He brought the saliva back to his work lab where it would go through the process, much like snake venom, of being injected into a horse, a rabbit and a sheep, in order to produce the antivenom.

And what do you know, but it eventually worked.

It has been five months and Robert LaChance should have been dead at least a couple of months ago. But he is alive; living proof that there is an antidote to the *zombivirus.*

And he now spends his time milking zombie saliva. Because they learned, not too long after his own antivenom saved his life, that there's something to do with various blood types of the infected zombies. You don't need to have the saliva of the zombie that bit you. All you need is the saliva from a matching blood type.

He might just go down in the history books, along with medical pioneers like Madame Curie or Alexander Fleming.

So he's out there, teaching people how to milk saliva from zombies. They call him the *Zombie Whisperer.*

For the masses, he might be seen as a genius who came up with the cure for a terrible zombie affliction.

But me, I'll never forget the sight of him that night, the determined look on his face, as he held the shot glass filled with Simone's saliva in one hand, his other hand clasped tightly around the wad of hundred dollar bills in his other, and the wry grin on his face as he looked at his pals and said. "I won the bet, bitches. I won!"

This Time Around

This time I woke to find myself sprawled naked in the grass, my shoulder nestled in a shrub and the coppery aftertaste of blood in my mouth. It was a cool morning, but humid, the unmistakable scent of the Hudson River hanging in the air.

I pulled my aching body into a sitting position and checked it over for injuries. Apart from the usual scrapes and scratches there was a nasty looking wound in my thigh. It hurt like it was no more than a bad bruise, but it looked like a bullet hole. I ran my hand down the leg and stuck my finger inside. Yes indeed, it was a bullet hole - the bullet was nestled just about an inch deep.

At least the bullet wasn't silver - now *that* I would have felt.

So to sum up my situation, there was a distinct taste of blood in my mouth and a bullet wound in my leg.

What the hell had I done this time?

I took a look around me. The park I was in was on the Hudson; that I could tell from the scent of the water. The early morning mist revealed beautiful Lady Liberty to me in teasing glimpses. Okay, so this was Battery Park. I was on the south western tip of Manhattan Island. And since I was currently a guest at the Algonquin Hotel in Mid-Town, getting three quarters of the way across this island bare naked was going to be one hell of a chore.

Uncovering the mystery of what exactly I'd been up to during last night's full moon, would, of course, be another.

But I was a mystery writer after all; and was usually able to piece it all together upon examination of the evidence. My memories as a wolf were scattered and non-linear snatches of smells, sounds, tastes, feelings and sights, not often available to my human conscious mind. Trying to piece them together in my conscious mind often gave me a migraine. I'd always thought perhaps that was how I'd preserved my sanity.

Unfortunately, with my growing popularity as a mystery writer, it was becoming easier for people to recognize me - at least in human form, that is. Finding a picture of myself scampering about the city butt naked on the cover of the tabloids was not a pleasant thought.

Was it time to move out of New York?

No, after all, growing up reading Spider-Man comic books, I'd always wanted to live here. So I was living my childhood dream. In my dreams, though, I'd been the wall-crawler, swinging around the city rooftops and nabbing the bad guys - I'd never dreamed that I would be one of the monsters that Spider-Man often faced down, like that astronaut who, wearing a moon rock on a chain around his neck was afflicted with the curse of the werewolf - something to do with wolves and the moon, I guess. But other than the concept of a full moon and werewolves, it never made sense to me. After all, everyone knows that being bitten by a werewolf is the way that a person becomes inflicted with the curse.

For me, it was a chance encounter with a wolf on a camping/hitchhiking trip through Upstate New York that led to my lycanthropic affliction.

The wolf had leapt from the bushes at the side of the highway just as a car came around the distant bend. With a failed attempt to abort the attack in mid-leap, its teeth nipped at my upraised right arm as it landed on me, the teeth barely sinking below the surface of my flesh. I fell back onto the road with the weight of the wolf hitting me on the chest, and the wolf quickly bounced off me and across the highway, rather than tear out my throat in one single gesture. I'd later learned that wolves do not kill for sport, but for food and for territory. The attack on me must have been an attempt at food that night, because if the goal had been to just kill me, it would have been over. The goal to consume me wasn't something the wolf could do with the car approaching, so it simply aborted the attack and ran - likely on to find a bird, rabbit or squirrel.

The driver, of course, didn't see the wolf attack, just that I'd been lying on the highway. He picked me up, a salesman eager to have someone to talk to - his incidental saving of my life was nothing more than a fortunate side-effect of his finding a driving companion. After hearing me tell him about the wolf attack that had nearly taken my life, he made the comment "pretty scary" and then regaled me with tales of his travels, facts about the Empire State and his goals for retirement.

Because we were heading in the same direction and he was thirsty for company, I ended up bunking with him at the hotel when he stayed for the night, he being eager to have me sleep in the chair in his own hotel room as his conversational prostitute.

And I'd ended up riding with him all the way in to New York City.

I'd stayed with him again upon our arrival into the city, engaging in another marathon conversation session in his hotel room. And, although he was a little peculiar, I couldn't help but like this man, not only because he'd accidentally saved my life, but also because of the incredible knowledge he would disperse, all with the innocence and wondrous thirst of a child.

Fortunately, he also knew the city well, so it was a good initiation to the city for me to spend my first night there with him.

Actually, Buddy (that's his name) and I became friends, and he visits me every time he returns to the city, usually for dinner, some drinks, and long conversations - the one-sided kind he is so enamored with - well into the wee hours of the night.

And, although Buddy never really asked me all that much about me and my personal life, he remembered how we'd met during the wolf attack. So, he often greeted me with the nickname "Wolfman" never knowing how close he really was to the truth.

I'd been in the city for almost three weeks before my first experience of lycanthropy. After getting over the fact of understanding what had happened to me and the reality of living with it, I found it desperately hard to hold a job. Sure, I wanted to be a writer - but I had to secure some sort of job to keep an income. And holding the types of jobs I was skilled for, being a waiter or a delivery driver, was often difficult. Waking up naked far from home usually left me late for work. Never-mind the times that I'd destroyed my uniform when turning into a wolf before I had the chance to get home and undress. And trying to avoid the night shift for several days in a row every month by calling in sick often left my employer with another good reason to fire me.

It wasn't until I was about six months into my curse that I'd discovered I could put my wolf-blood to good use. Since becoming a werewolf, my human self retained some of the benefits of my wolfish nature. My senses were all heightened - I no longer needed to wear glasses, for example - and my strength had seemed to double, sometimes quadruple, depending on the proximity of the full-moon.

My ability to heal also dramatically improved and my constitution has never been better. I haven't had a cold or caught a flu virus since becoming a werewolf.

So while it's not a glamorous life, it's not all entirely bad.

My extra strength and immune system allowed me to work the more dangerous labor jobs that paid well and most people couldn't stay at long. Then, later, once building more of a nest egg, I was able move up within the companies I worked for, by being able to see and hear things that normal people missed out on. In essence, my EQ and ability to interact with and influence people was dramatically improved. I was able to pull off this incredible charisma.

It's how I was able to get an editor to agree to read my first novel.

Along those same lines, the heightened senses allowed me to more properly explore the senses when writing descriptions in a novel, thus improving my writing style and ability to draw readers right into the scene.

It's probably why I was such a successful mystery writer.

With the success came appearances on talk shows and the occasional red carpet type of event, such as when one of my novels had been turned into a feature film. Recognition came with that success, making it harder for me to simply blend into the crowd.

Yes, even in New York, where the extraordinary seemed commonplace, it was hard for a naked celebrity to just blend into the scenery.

Not that I wasn't used to having to find new ways to sneak back home naked after a night of howling at the moon, but the celebrity aspect was starting to make the task of not being recognized that much more difficult.

After quickly determining that there were no humans nearby in the narrow sliver of park I was in, I decided to take the time to remove the bullet from my leg. If I didn't it would be lodged inside. The bleeding had already stopped and the wound had already started to heal, so I could tell it was at least a few hours old. By the end of the day, the healing, I knew, would be well advanced, and by the day after the next the scab might even by ready to fall off. Not that I often let the scabs fall off on their own. I relished picking at them.

I was able to pry the wound open enough to snag the bullet fragment between the tip of my index finger and my thumbnail. After a minute or so of twisting and prying, it slipped right out.

I couldn't very well walk around with a bullet lodged in my thigh. The thought of setting off metal detectors, now almost as common as pay phones used to be, wasn't all that appealing to me.

Getting up, I flung the bullet fragment into the murky depths of the Hudson.

It was now time to make my way back home.

Judging by the sun's position in the sky and the sounds of traffic, it was likely some time after 5:30 AM. The sun had just come up maybe ten or fifteen minutes ago, but it being an August morning, the humidity and smog hung in the air like a light morning fog.

The first significant set of commuters would likely be arriving on the 6:20 AM Staten Island Ferry. The Ferry landed just south of where I was now. If I were able to find at least some of the right clothes, I could perhaps blend in with those folks and make my way to the subway. Provided I could get a handful of change I'd be able to take the subway. If not, I had a long walk ahead of me. And, despite my healing ability and the slightly thicker padding on my feet now, walking that many miles in my bare feet on pavement and concrete still wasn't pleasant.

I paused to survey the park in a little more detail and pick up on the scents around me, at least the ones that weren't the usual typical background scents here, such as the grass, the sap from the trees and the cigarette butts. There was the smell of semen mingled with latex, from a condom that I could see now that I'd sensed it, about three yards to my right, just beneath a park bench. Near it I could see a newspaper, smell the newsprint, the stale remnants of cheap cologne, the smell of vaginal juices and the bitter dregs left behind in a coffee cup lying on its side. But I could smell another distinct vaginal scent that wasn't obscured by latex coming from the vicinity. I started walking in that direction.

On the other side of a tree near the bench, and out of the line of sight from where I'd originally stood, there was a pair of pink panties. That's where the vaginal juice smell was coming from. I headed over and picked the panties up, judging whether or not I'd be able to fit into them.

It's amazing what people throw away and in what places. While the origin of these panties seemed obvious to me based on the other evidence - a pair of lovers had likely enjoyed each other in the dark on this bench - I'd always wondered, for example, why you sometimes see a single shoe on the side of the highway or on the side of a road. Who throws out such articles of clothing and why there? I'd never met anyone in all my travels who admitted to losing or throwing away a single shoe while in a vehicle or traveling - so why, in all my time, was it such a common sight?

A mystery to solve another day I thought as I bent over, muttered "Desperate time," and stepped into the panties and pulled them up my legs.

Fortunately they had a good bit of play in them, so, though snug, I was able to pull them on.

It was a start at least.

I kept walking in that same direction, feeling I was on a roll.

Maybe I'd even find a pair of shoes in my size. Perhaps a nice set of cherry red pumps with stiletto heels.

As I was walking, a snippet of memory from last night came to me. *The squeal of tires and brakes and a bright, painful flash of headlight beams.* The sudden memory burst stopped me in my tracks. The memory flashed through my mind again, this time *the smell of rubber burning, overtop of a stronger background fishy smell,* then the memory was gone again. I pawed at it tentatively, but couldn't bring anything else back.

Instead I started thinking about the last memory I had as a human last night.

I was staying at the Algonquin Hotel. Ever since that one novel of mine was made into a blockbuster movie two and a half years ago, the rest of my novels had been republished and the royalties started screaming in. With the advance from the movie rights having been socked away into a secure investment, and with all the extra cash coming in, I finally abandoned my Chelsea bachelor apartment, and decided to take up residence at the Algonquin Hotel.

The Algonquin, of course, known for its literary history.

If I could live out my childhood dream of living in New York and being a writer like Stan Lee, the genius who'd created Spider-Man, I could live out a later adult fantasy in which I was a writer-in-residence of sorts at this spot.

The management was able to cut me enough of a deal for the long-term room, and I made frequent appearances within the lobby, where the cultural elite liked to hang out before Broadway shows or the Opera. I didn't mind hanging out there myself, and it was a thrill to be part of the ambiance. After all, it was the ambiance of the lobby area of the Algonquin that had attracted me in the first place.

So last night, after a productive writing session, I'd headed out for an early evening stroll. I thought I would have enough time to get to Central Park, where I often liked to be before a change. Being locked up in a hotel room as a wolf wasn't a good thing, not if you wanted to stay in the good books with hotel management. Besides, I liked to also ensure that I gave my other-half a good outing, the ability to run and expend all that pent-up energy in a healthy way.

When I was planning on doing a Central Park outing, I often stashed clothes nearby in the park for when I awoke. I had to, of course, keep finding new places to stash my clothes because of the times when I returned to find my clothes missing. It's amazing at how quickly certain homeless folks can be at finding things you would have thought were well hidden.

By then, of course, I'd stopped having to also stash a set of keys or a wallet or I.D. or anything like that. One of the benefits of living at the Algonquin was that the Concierge knew me and I could get in and up to my room without any hassle whenever I didn't have my key or I.D.

Last night, however, I don't remember even making it to Central Park.

It was evening, the sun was setting. I'd left the Algonquin wearing a pair of disposable clothes and with my extra change of clothes stashed in a plastic grocery bag - no, I didn't like to get naked before the change and thus save the clothes I was in - so, I wore either older or cheap discount store clothing on "change" nights.

I was walking up 5th Avenue towards the park ...

... and that's where my human memory fails. The wolf-related amnesia I suffered from typically struck anywhere from five to fifteen minutes before and after a transition. That told me it's possible I didn't even make it to Central Park before I changed.

The other clue I had was the fact that, when I made the change in Central Park, my wolf-self very often didn't leave the boundaries of the park. With plenty of places to run, cavort and hunt down prey of the rodent and other small animal variety, there was little reason for my wolf-self to leave the park.

Consumed in the memories and the attempt at regurgitating the events of last night, I almost failed to detect the scent of another human just downwind to my right. It was a single person, a man, and his scent was coming from around the corner of the building on State Street where the people from the Staten Island ferry came in - the scent was getting stronger as he approached.

I glanced down at myself, clad in the flimsy and tight pink panties, then to the left and right. There was no place for me to hide. It was too late to duck under cover.

I could only hope that this person wasn't one of my fans.

Based on the unfamiliar scent, I knew this was a person I hadn't met before - that was something at least. There was also the slight tinge of ammonia or a similar cleaning agent on this person, so my initial thought was that this might be one of the cleaners leaving the Wall Street office towers after a busy night of work.

He stopped as I rounded the corner, and there he stood, about five and a half feet tall. He had a large round face, receding hairline and a few untendered wisps of long, unshaven hair on his lower chin. His eyes were almond shaped and a very bright blue. He wore a red plaid shirt and bright yellow suspenders to hold up his brown pleated slacks. Over that he wore a thin windbreaker jacket. On his feet he wore these long red sneakers, and his stance was such that his feet were angled outwards, the way you sometimes see a clown standing.

He smiled at me. A huge, unabashed full tooth smile and said in a loud and deep voice, not unlike one a game show announcer might use to call the next contestant on stage from the audience. "Lovely morning, isn't it!"

Not one double-take for the way I was dressed.

Yeah, I know, I know, this is New York after all. But still, you'd expect at least a slight pause. And, even in the average New Yorker used to seeing the strange relatively regularly, I would expect to smell at least the slightest twinge of fear. After all, a strange man in a pair of tight pink panties wandering the streets typically signaled that something was amiss.

Before I could say anything, he asked: "Do you happen to have the time?" He said this in the same loud announcer-type voice. It was obviously a planned and well-practiced line.

I instinctively glanced at my bare wrist and then took another look at him. He was wearing a watch.

Then I understood. It explained the well-rehearsed line, which was a little conversation starter, something it was okay for one stranger to ask of another. This poor guy was a little slow. But he certainly wasn't living on the street - he had a clean, recently bathed smell to him. My instincts kicked in, knowing he was a person who required adult supervision, protection. So, either he was lost, having wandered out of a protected area, or his supervisory support was nearby. I knew the second option couldn't be right, because I would have smelled another person in the vicinity. And I could tell that he and I were the only people outside within about a one block radius.

"I'm sorry," I told him. "I don't have the time, but I think I can guess."

His eyes lit up. This was going to be a game of sorts. He raised his wrist and looked at his own watch. "Okay, then you guess. And I'll tell you if you're right. I'm Wally."

"Hi Wally. I'm Michael. So, Wally, if I guess correctly, what sort of prize is that worth?"

"Prize?" he asked. Again, he wasn't trepidatious in the slightest. His scent revealed playfulness and wonder.

"Yeah," I said. "I'm a little short of clothes here. Maybe you could help by lending me some clothing if I guess correctly. Like, maybe your jacket."

Immediately fear fused out of him. But he didn't step back. He wasn't afraid of me, but of something else. A consequence of the thought of giving away his clothes? "No," he said quietly. "Can't do that. Can't do that. Ma says that I need to keep track of my things, like my clothes. Have to keep track of them. Can't do that."

"Okay, okay, maybe you could help me find some clothes."

The fear was immediately replaced with the playfulness again, and deeper excitement. "Okay," he nodded.

"Speaking of your Ma, Wally, where is she?"

His scent got frightened again, but also worried and concerned and confused. "She's on the ferry. I stopped to tie my shoes and watched an ant walking right through all the people. Then I caught up with Ma again, but I started to worry about the ant. I ran back to him, to make sure nobody had stepped on him. I didn't hear the ferry man announce the gate was closing. I couldn't find the ant, but I kept looking. Then Ma was calling for me, and the ferry was leaving. So I'm waiting here for Ma. I still can't find the ant, so I started walking to find him. I saw other ants, but not the one I had seen before. Still can't find him."

"It's okay, Wally. I'm sure that the ant is okay. And your Ma saw you on the dock, didn't she?"

"Yes. She was calling to me."

"She's probably going to be on the next ferry."

"You think so?"

"Of course," and then my nurturing instinct kicked in slightly higher. It suddenly seemed likely to me that Wally's mother was a cleaning lady with neither the family support nor the money to afford someone to look after her son while she worked. So she likely did what she had to - adhere him to the same schedule as her, working throughout the night and sleeping in the morning.

"And I'll stay here with you until she does." Of course, it would certainly be tricky for me to not be seen by anybody dressed the way I was, but I'd deal with that when the time came.

"Okay," he said. "But do we still get to find some clothes for you?"

"Sure," I smiled. Then I caught the scent of someone approaching from what seemed to be South Street. It was a man, not quite as clean smelling as Wally, but not so unwashed as to be a street person. Also, he wasn't wearing cologne or after shave, so it wasn't likely a business person.

"Wally, listen," I said. "Someone is coming. And I'm ... a little shy about people not seeing me dressed the way I am. So I'm just going to hide. I'll still be nearby, though, okay."

"Okay," he said.

Just a few yards to the west there was a series of concrete barricades, due to construction that was going on with the pier and docking station. I quickly bounded in that direction, easily leapt over the barricade and ducked down behind it.

As I'd ducked down, I was struck with another memory from my last stint as a wolf. This time it was the deafening roar of a gunshot and the unmistakable smell of gunpowder; a flash of pain in my leg and somewhere, muffled, in the background a child-like voice that said something like: "No, not the nice doggie!"

I shook my head - now wasn't the time to have a flashback - and focused on Wally and the approaching stranger.

The footsteps got closer as the scent became stronger.

"Well, what do we have here?" a voice called out. It was deeper in tone than Wally's and spoken in a loud, carefully pronounced way. The accent was different in pitch, not the same New York/Brooklyn flavor of speech common to this area, but more like my own accent, which had a New England ring to it.

"Good morning." Wally said, and then, in his announcer voice said: "Would you happen to have the time?"

"The time?" the stranger responded in a sneering tone. "You're the one wearing a watch, dude." There was a pause. "Oh, I get it, you're a retard."

"My Ma says that it's not nice to use that word." Again, Wally's scent wasn't fearful, it was indignant, offended.

"Well your Ma isn't here to stop me, now, is she bub?"

"Uh, no, my Ma is on the ferry."

"I see." There was another pause. "Okay, man, give me your watch."

"Oh no." The fear became obvious this time not only in Wally's scent but in the way his voice broke when he continued to speak. "Can't do that. Ma says that I need to keep track of my things, like my clothes and my watch."

I stood up at that point. The stranger was facing away from me. He was about my height, wearing faded jeans and a crew-cut t-shirt. He had long greasy blond hair that covered the sides of his face. Wally didn't notice that I'd moved. His eyes never left the man in front of him. I quickly stepped onto the barricade and down onto the other side then strode quietly towards the two.

"I don't give a rat's ass what your Ma says." The stranger said, his finger jabbing at Wally's chest as he leaned in closer to my friend. "I said 'hand over that watch.' And let me see your wallet while we're at it." I was just a few steps away and gaining ground quickly.

"Can't do that." Wally said, his heart racing. "Can't do that. Can't do that. Can't do that."

The stranger grabbed Wally's wrist and pulled him closer, his angle changing enough that he spotted me from the corner of his eye.

His head turned in my direction. "What the hell do you want?" he said, his scent revealing a slight bit of fear, and then, after a brief double take in seeing the way I was dressed, he melted into a grin, his scent reeked of confidence and in the same sneering voice he'd used before, said: "Oh, another retard. But it looks like someone already got your stuff. Nice panties, dude!" He started laughing.

"I'll give you one warning," I said in a calm and quiet voice. "Leave him alone or you'll regret it."

As I spoke the words, the man's confidence started to waver. He immediately maneuvered behind Wally, taking Wally's right arm and bending it up against his back. Wally's face gave off a look of pain that I could smell off of him too. That really bothered me.

"Back off buddy," he said, his free hand coming up with a knife. He pressed the blade against Wally's throat.

"Michael, help me," Wally said. "Can't get blood on my clothes. Can't. Ma will be upset and think I can't take care of my things."

"Shut up!" the stranger said

It was the split second he was distracted when I made my move. One hand going for his throat, the other for the hand holding the knife. He didn't stand a chance. By the time he noticed I'd moved, I'd already had a firm grip on his throat with my left hand while I knocked the knife out of his left mitt with my right.

After disarming him, I thrust my right hand up and with a quick palm jab, broke his nose.

He stumbled back a couple of steps, blood gushing from his nose.

I moved forward and gave his chest a push. He fell back on his ass, his hands furtively trying to stop the blood pumping from his nostrils, his eyes wide - he looked more like a kid that had been eating from a bowl of strawberries and got caught, his lips and cheeks coated in red and these wide "oh shit" eyes.

I let out a low, deep laugh which was part growl.

That's when the confusion I smelled off him turned to an ice cold fear.

Behind me, Wally's scent still revealed fear.

"Oh no, Michael. He's got blood all over his shirt. His Ma is going to be upset now."

"That's okay," I told Wally as I reached down and grabbed this guy by the hair. "His Ma knows that he's a bad boy."

He didn't resist me, he just whined and held onto my hand as I lifted him off of the ground and put him down on the other side of me. I gave him a quick kick with the side of my foot, knocking the wind out of him, and whispered for him not to struggle if he knew what was good for him.

I started walking in the direction of Battery Park, dragging this would-be mugger behind me by lifting him into the air and setting him down hard, almost as if he were a short, fetal-like walking stick. He let out a forced puff of air each time he connected with the ground. "I'll be right back, Wally," I called out over my shoulder.

I carry-dragged the man to the first set of bushes and told him to take his own clothes off.

"L-leave me alone. Please don't rape me," he whimpered, and then for good measure, because he had to ensure I knew he was a tough guy. "Y-you f-fag."

"I'm not going to rape you, you little freak. Just take your shirt and pants off. I need your clothes, you dipshit. And you need to be taught a lesson."

A few minutes later, I emerged from the bush with this guy over my shoulder. His pants fit me okay, but his shirt was too bloody to wear. I'd torn it into strips and used a few of them to tie his hands behind his back. It had been nice to discard those panties finally, but I let him keep his underwear, which he was still wearing. I had stuffed the panties into his mouth to keep him from yelling out and secured it into place with another strip of his shirt.

Closer to a bus stop on State Street, where he was sure to be visible to thousands of morning commuters within the next hour, I tied this fellow, standing, to the post, and, using his own fresh blood wrote "BULLY" on his chest. Before I left I told him I'd be watching him and if he ever tried to take advantage of someone like he had this morning, I'd show up out of nowhere and hurt and humiliate him in more ways than he could imagine.

The distinct smell of fresh urine overpowered the strong scent of his latest wave of fear.

Wally walked over to me, studying the writing on this thug's chest but ensuring he didn't get too close. His head twisted to the side, I could tell that he couldn't make out the writing.

"Are you okay, Wally?" I asked.

"Ayuh," Wally said, still distracted by this stranger. "Michael, he's a bad man, isn't he?"

"He sure is. But we don't need to worry about him any more, Wally. C'mon, let's go wait for your Mom to get back."

"Okay,"

On our walk over we could see the next ferry coming in, about 100 yards off shore. I fell into place behind Wally and studied the scent coming off of him. Mingled with his own scent and the ammonia was another person's. Similar, but tinged with a feminine perfume. It was his mother's scent, subtle, but there - as if she'd given him a tight hug in the space of the last couple of hours.

I walked as close to the end of the dock as I could and waited for the wind to shift. Mingled with the scent of the sea water, the fumes from the ferry and the multiple passengers, I couldn't pick up Wally's mother's scent, but I could detect that ammonia smell.

I turned to my friend. "She's on this ferry, Wally."

"She is?"

"Yes, she'll be docking in a few minutes. I'm going to leave you now. You stay here, okay."

"Okay." His eyes turned sad and he gave off the scent of disappointment. "Do you have to go, Michael?"

"I do, Wally. I have some place I need to be."

"Okay," he stepped toward me and gave me a big hug. "G'bye, Michael."

I gently chuckled at his honest outward show of affection - how rare a thing between men in today's society. The world needs more people like Wally. "Goodbye, my friend."

I turned and walked away, keeping track of him easily enough due to the shift in wind. When I'd walked about half a block, I turned to see that the ferry was docking. I could hear a woman's voice calling out to Wally and Wally responding. I felt assured that he was safely out of harm's way.

I quickened my pace, and started walking up State Street.

I needed to get more distance covered before rush hour, when the chance of being spotted became more of a threat. Well, at least I had pants now. And it was a summer day, not all that outrageous to be walking around without a shirt on.

But still.

When walking up Broadway, near Liberty Street I was overwhelmed with a flood of sensory memory. I know that it has been a dozen years since the tragic events of September 11th, 2001, but I swear I can still smell and taste the acrid smell of electrical fire, the jet fuel, the ash consisting of burnt flesh, concrete, paper, wood plastics and asbestos that I smelled in the days, weeks and months following the disaster. It was several years before I was able to approach this area from within about 10 blocks without being overcome with not just the smell and taste in the air, but with the horrific memories that went with each sensation.

Even now, though I swear I can still detect subtle hints of those scents and tastes in the air, I'm sure it's my mind that conjures it all back to full power. However, even now, there is no mistaking the very clear smell of utter despair that lingers in the air. Even years later, there continue to be an endless parade of tourists and visitors to the city who seek out the infamous landmark of Ground Zero; and they feed the area with this lasting olfactory image that constantly threatens to burn itself into my very psyche like a image burned onto a cathode ray tube.

Needless to say, I was glad to move past that tragic landmark.

I'd made it about three blocks north when the morning rush hour traffic started to really take form. That's when I remembered my appointment with Mack Wilson. Mack was my literary agent, a tough old codger who always had a cigar hanging out of the side of his mouth (recently more unlit than lit due to the city smoking by-laws) and an insulting quip at the ready.

Mack was a guy with a crusty surface and a good heart. He was a tough negotiation scrapper, and I was always glad he was fighting on my side. I'd be afraid to face him down even as a wolf.

One thing I didn't ever want to do, however, was piss Mack off for no reason. He was a punctual man who lived by a certain sense of old fashioned honor and principles such as "a man always honors his commitments" and "a man is only as good as his weakest words" - they always reminded me of the moral that Spider-Man learned in his very first adventure, that *with great power comes great responsibility*. God bless Stan Lee for delivering such basic wisdom in a format that could be easily digested by my young mind and yet continue to guide me throughout my adult life.

In any case, Mack and I had a breakfast appointment, and seeing a few folks in their business and power suits hustling into and out of cabs and office tower entrances, reminded me of Mack and the fact that we were supposed to be meeting in about an hour at the Metro Market just one street up from The Algonquin.

Considering where I was and the time I had to get home and change, I wasn't panicked; but I was realistically concerned. I mean, hoofing it by foot all the way was no longer an option unless I started running at top speed now and ran the entire distance. It could be done, but it would be very obvious - I mean, a man in jogging shorts, running shoes and a headband, sure I could get away with that - but not shoeless and shirtless in a pair of worn and dirty jeans. That would just be begging some flatfoot beat cop or patrol car to stop me. At least my bullet wound was covered now, but still, being noticed even that much would not be a good thing.

I needed to get some sort of vehicular transportation back up to Mid-Town.

The morning rush hour crowd was starting to fill out, and it would now be more difficult for me to elude detection. At a diner that already had a line-up down the street, I walked over to the a-frame style street sign and hefted it up and over my shoulders, wearing it like a sandwich board.

I started calling out "Eat at Charlie's Diner" in a monotone voice, and kept walking down the street and around the next block. Sure enough, the faces started to pay no attention to me.

Good old New Yorkers. All you needed to do to get people to ignore you was to try to get their attention.

God, I loved this city.

Another flash of memory from the night before struck me at that point. *The low howl of a siren as the scenery quickly flashed by in a blur. I was running, chasing another four-legged creature that was moving as fast as I could move. The scent ahead of me was confusingly much like the scent of another wolf, which made no sense.*

I shook my head and tried to drudge the memory back again.

All that returned was *the blur of the alley walls as I rushed past them and the two-toned whine of the approaching police siren.*

I'd made it about three blocks in this fashion when I finally encountered the scent of someone who seemed intrigued by the sign I was wearing. What I mean is that the curious nature was obvious, but there was a lingering scent of another emotion - desire.

Basically, somebody who'd spotted me wanted this sign for themselves.

I started panning the faces of the people nearby. Across the street and about half a block ahead of me sitting on the curb was an older woman in a long trench coat and faded green slacks. Mingled with her emotive scents was the smell of stale sweat and recent flatulence. Spotting her, I smiled and carefully crossed the street.

She held onto the shopping cart beside her - strategically stacked with an assortment of odds and ends several feet higher than the metal cage sides - with a firm clutching grip. It was apparent that you wouldn't be able to pry her fingers from that cart until she had been dead for several minutes.

She stood as I got within a few feet of her, still not letting go of her cart and grinned a wry, gap toothed smile at me.

"Nice sign, Cookie." She cackled with a bit of a slur. Fortunately for her, she'd been able to score some alcohol recently. After gaining my special sensory abilities, I was better able to understand others whose perceptions I couldn't quite grasp before. I found myself doing a lot less judging of people now, and simply accepted people for who they were. And, if alcohol helped her cope with the stress of what her day and her life was, then so be it.

"Thanks," I said, able to immediately detect that she was in a mood for bartering. As I stood close to her, it was a bit more difficult to filter out her vodka breath, the sour-milk body odor smell and get through to her emotive scents. "Care to make a trade?"

Her grin spread and she took her right hand off of her cart momentarily to run her palms together before clutching it once more.

"You don't happen to have a shirt my size in that cart of yours, do you?" I smiled.

She paused and glanced at the cart, her head tilting to one side. I could smell that she did have what I was looking for. "I might," she said. "What else you got."

"C'mon, lady." I said, throwing my arms up with my palms out. "Look at what I'm wearing here. I've got nothing but this sign and my pants."

"Not sure if that's a good deal for me, Cookie" she mused, but I could tell she was bluffing. It was as obvious to me as the fact that she'd just released a silent, but foul packet of flatulence into her pants. She still desperately wanted my sign.

"Fine," I said, starting to turn around. "See you later."

I made it about three steps, all the while smelling her anxiety growing exponentially.

"Wait a minute, Cookie! Wait a minute!"

*** ***

Five minutes later I was walking away from our transaction wearing a slightly torn dress shirt that was a size too large for me and missing two buttons as well as a pair of mismatched shoes, one of which was a perfectly fitting sandal, the other was a sneaker that was a size too large, but with a torn sock stuffed in front of my toes, it fit okay.

Getting there, I told myself, and thought about Mack waiting for me at the Metro Market. I briefly considered my next step. Perhaps it should be to get a quarter so I could make a phone call to his cell phone and let him know that I was running late. But that thought was quickly dismissed given how I knew he detested such dalliances. Mack had the patience of a toddler and, despite the fact that I was now making him some pretty decent money, he wouldn't put up with a client that made him wait a single minute for an appointment. In his point of view, if a client couldn't be bothered to be on time for a meeting, he wouldn't waste another second working on their behalf.

I realized I was very fortunate to have found an agent like Mack, and while I'd be able to get another agent without issue, I found myself needing him - not just for business reasons, but for personal ones as well. Like Buddy, he was quirky but interesting, and he constantly challenged me. I found myself needing to be challenged in my personal relationships - if you didn't have to work hard at something, it almost didn't seem worth it.

And I definitely had to work hard to be in Mack's good books.

And that's where I wanted to stay.

I moved to Murray Street towards the subway entrance. I figured I'd be able to sneak onto the subway, but only with the additional thought that the next time I took the subway, I'd pay double to make up for my free ride.

Sure, a lot of people would make fun of me for trying to live my life so straight. But the person who I had to please most was myself, and, in the same way that Mack was true to himself, I set my own personal standards high for a good reason. After all, I was the one who had to live with the consequences of my actions.

And having blackouts of my time as a wolf was the hardest thing to deal with, particularly after waking up the way I had this morning. I mean, if I'd hurt an innocent person, or even worse, killed someone, I'm not sure how I'd be able to live with that.

A foggy string of memory from last night filtered up to my conscious mind. This time, the memory was completely non-visual, but I could tell I was *moving fast through an alley from the rapid patter of my paws on the pavement. I was chasing the wolf ahead of me. And, mingled with his hot breath was the distinct scent of human blood* - the same human blood that I woke up tasting.

A blaring horn to my immediate left broke the wispy memory. I glared at the driver as I continued walking towards the subway entrance.

So, there was another wolf.

What was I doing chasing him?

Yes, him, I knew it was a 'him' from the memory of his scent. That and the stink of human mingling with the canine scent meant that, like me, he was a werewolf. What else did I know? He had the blood on him that I'd tasted when I woke up.

This was getting curiouser and curiouser.

I moved down the stairs, starting to mesh in with the morning rush hour hustle, and, in the midst of the crowd, I was easily able to check for observant eyes and hop over the turnstile and make my way, virtually un-noticed except by a few people who'd been immediately behind me, down to the lower platform level. I shuffled through the crowd over to the far left of the platform, to ensure I "lost" the people who'd spotted me, just in case.

The rumbling of an approaching northbound train could be heard down the tunnel - this was good - I'd be able to make good time and get back to the hotel with enough time to get inside, have a quick shower, change, then be downstairs and around the block to meet Mack.

That's when I heard the faint gasp and brief cry for help amidst a scuffling.

I glanced at the approaching light of the train, then swiveled my head around, looking down the platform where I'd heard the cry come from. There was a balding middle aged man in a grey suit surrounded by three goons all dressed in the same blue jeans, black t-shirts and red bandanas. They were either part of some gang, all had the same fashion consultant, or spent so much of their time stealing and vandalizing that they didn't give much time or thought to their own personal style. I was betting on the latter.

A glint of light from the blade of one of the men caught my eye as he waved his weapon, saying "I said, hand it over now."

The other two men flanked the bald man, each holding him by the upper arm.

"Aw crap," I mumbled, moving down the platform towards them - I was going to miss my train for sure.

"Hey!" I called out as I started rushing toward the melee. Behind me, the train arrived at the station.

The leader immediately turned to face me, bringing his knife in my direction as well. His lackeys also turned their attention toward me, which achieved the first of my goals.

I continued rushing the leader, and, just as I got within striking distance, he thrust the blade at me. I easily dodged the blade and him with a full body tackle, my left elbow raised to connect with his face.

His nose crunched noisily and he actually caught a bit of air, trailing behind a thin stream of blood from his nose. His head connected with the wall first, his head making a satisfying hollow bong sound against the tile before he crumpled to the floor. I kicked the knife he'd dropped down to the track level just as the train started to pull out. Blocking the noise of the train, I focused on the sound of his heartbeat. It was still strong and steady; he was unconscious and relatively healthy, despite the smashed nose and bruised noggin.

The lackey on the man's left let go of his prey and rushed me while I was partially turned away. Given the setup, I could have easily used his momentum to flip him over my back and send him sprawling to the track level. But my goal wasn't to kill, merely to subdue.

Yes, I behaved more like a wolf and less like human every day.

I ducked under his rush, sending a right jab into his gut. My punch easily lifted him off of the ground, breaking a couple of ribs and knocking the breath out of him. As his feet came back onto the ground, I shoved him in the direction of his buddy and he stumbled, as if drunk, in a forward run, trying, vainly, to get his balance.

The buddy pushed his captive forward and ducked to the side. The man in the grey suit let out a moan as he collided with the incoming body, and he and the second goon piled to the floor in a mass of limbs.

I easily vaulted over the two, who lay there like lovers having just finished their business, grabbed the third attacker - who tried vainly to avoid my grasp by the scruff of his collar and slammed him, headfirst into the wall. He went down like last call at a frat bar.

At that point I offered a hand to the man in the grey suit who was now starting to catch his breath from the hit he had taken. He took my hand and I helped him to his feet

"T-thanks," he said, his eyes darting back and forth between the man he had just been laying in a pile on the floor with and the two who lay sprawled on the floor against the wall, as if nervous that they'd be getting up.

"Don't worry," I said. "They won't be going anywhere any time soon."

He looked over at me, as if seeing me for the first time, and did a double take. I wondered if he might be a fan of mine, recognizing who I really was, as he stood there, staring at me, his mouth agape.

Then he stepped forward, his voice low and gentle. "Listen. I'd like to thank you for helping me out."

"My pleasure," I said. I glanced around. Most of the morning commuters that had been on the platform with us had boarded the last train. However, a few people who'd gotten off this train and more people coming in from the street were milling around, just a few steps away, curiously looking at us and the unconscious men. I was eager for the next train to arrive and whisk me away from here.

"No, I mean it," he said, reaching in his back pocket and producing his wallet. He quickly thumbed it open and produced a twenty dollar bill. "Here. Maybe you can get yourself a warm meal."

I couldn't believe it. He thought I was a homeless person. But I couldn't blame him; after all, look at how I was dressed, how I smelled.

Dumbfounded, I tried to protest. "No, you don't need to ..."

"Please, it's the least I can do," he said, pulling out another twenty.

Just then, a commotion started near the stairs. Oh shit. Security. I couldn't afford to be held back answering questions about the scuffle. It looked like I wouldn't be taking the next train after all. Damn.

"Thanks," I mumbled, sheepishly taking the forty dollars. I started to walk away quickly. "The guards are coming now. You'll be safe."

I tried to blend into the nearest crowd. It didn't work so well because many people cleared a wide path for me. These must have been people who'd seen the commotion. As I got deeper into the crowd, though, fewer people moved out of my way, and I squeezed my way through them, making a wide birth of the stairs as two security guards rushed toward my friend in the grey suit.

Continuing to move against the incoming crowd, I made my way up the stairs and to the street. For good measure I ran at top speed for several blocks.

As I ran, my mind flashed back to running in the alley again.

Racing low through the dark alley, the wolf ahead of me, its scent, and the blood of the human mingled with it enticing me to run faster. Finally, approaching the end of the alley as it met a street, I tensed and lunged into the air, coming down with my fangs just shy of the other wolf's neck. We rolled and he broke free, turned and faced me. My next nip was at his mouth, and my taste buds were infused with the human blood that coated his tongue and maw.

I continued walking north, and was able to hail a cab by the time I reached Canal Street.

"The Algonquin Hotel," I said, climbing into the back of the taxi. "There's a twenty dollar tip in it for you if you can get there within half an hour."

"No prob," the driver said, a wry grin on his face. "This car can find streets that aren't on anyone else's map."

I wasn't sure exactly what that meant, but his comment did fill me with confidence.

As the cab raced up Broadway and turned right on Grand, I sat back in the seat and rested my head, realizing it was the first time I'd stopped since waking up.

I closed my eyes and tried to conjure up more memories from last night, but none came; just this low throbbing sensation behind my eyes. I should know better than to try to force the memories.

When I opened my eyes I saw there was a newspaper from the customer before me. New York Press. The large bold font headline read: "Vicious Wolf Attack Kills Man." The story mentioned a "pack of wolves" spotted running from the bloody scene where a homeless man was slaughtered. Police encountered the wolves near Fulton and Water, where shots were fired. An officer claims to have wounded at least one of the wolves, but the animals quickly fled the scene and have yet to turn up elsewhere. One witness commented that "it was as if the streets just swallowed them up."

Midway through the article I must have faded off, because the next thing I knew the cabbie was telling me we had arrived. It made sense that I was overtired since I didn't actually spend last night sleeping, but rather running through the city streets, attacking another wolf, and being shot at by the police. No, not just shot at, but actually shot. And, since this had been the first time I'd sat down all morning, my body, overcome with fatigue, did the natural thing.

Out of habit I glanced at my wrist, but there was no watch there.

"I got you here in just under twenty minutes." The cabbie said, shaking his head, his eyes closed and wreaking of a deep, deep pride. "Man, they said it couldn't be done. But every day, every single day, I prove them wrong."

"Much to my satisfaction," I said, handing him the two twenties and stepping out of the cab.

As he pulled away I realized I didn't have time to go inside, shower and get a change of clothes. I glanced at my reflection in the window of a van parked on the street. Okay, so I looked a little worse for wear. But I'd rather show up completely naked and with a giant turd on my head than to be late for a meeting with Mack.

As it was, once I walked down the street and around the block, I'd be just a few minutes early for our meeting, and that would be cutting it close enough.

Moving down the street, the sun now peeking through a break in the overcast sky, there was a slight spring in my step as I thought about what I would order for breakfast. At that thought my stomach growled.

In the back of my mind, I wondered when I might again meet that other wolf who was stalking in my territory. It was a mystery I'd likely solve some other time around, but at the thought of that other wolf, I growled.

It was a softer, quieter growl than the one my stomach had just made.

A Murder of Scarecrows

When Wilson Kendrick woke to the subtle yet distinct thump in the middle of the night, he threw aside the sheets and pattered across the chilled hardwood floor toward the window. He expected to see the Saundersons arriving home late from one of their semi-regular family trips to Maine; or perhaps the driver of a car stalled on the stretch of Highway 7 adjacent to his property.

What he saw in the pale moonlight, instead, were a dozen people scattered about the vast lawn, completely still and unmoving.

Squinting to make out details through the foggy darkness, he changed his mind.

It wasn't a group of people, it was a group of scarecrows.

No, not a group. The term commonly used for a group of crows came to mind.

It was a murder of scarecrows.

A shudder crawled up the base of his spine and cumulated in the reflexive shirking of his shoulder blades.

He stood at the window, not sure what he was going to do; uncertain what a person should do in such a circumstance.

He bided his time by squinting through the window and counting the still, silent sentinels in his yard.

There were thirteen of them.

Deciding he wasn't going to be able to get back to sleep, he took off his pyjamas and pulled on the pair of jeans and the neatly pressed t-shirt laid out on the trunk at the end of his bed.

Fully dressed, he walked back to the window to do another head count.

"One, two, three . . ." he counted quietly under his breath, his thin boney finger tapping the window pane as he moved it about pinpointing each still figure in the crosshairs of his vision, ". . . thirteen, fourteen, fifteen, sixteen."

Sixteen?

Something was wrong. He could see himself miscounting by one or two perhaps, but not by three.

He turned around and opened his bedside drawer for the pad of paper and a pencil which he kept to jot down his dreams whenever he woke in the middle of the night. Not that he'd used the pencil and notepad in months; a deep, relaxed sleeper, Wilson rarely remembered his dreams – he just felt good knowing it was there in the drawer, just in case.

He returned to the window and did a recount, this time placing a short mark on the page for each scarecrow he counted.

The count this time was eighteen.

"What's going on?"

He let out a short laugh as he realized what must be happening. A group of local kids must be having fun with him, playing a prank on the middle-aged stranger from out of town who'd moved into their neighborhood earlier that year. It was fall now and perhaps a town tradition to spook the new guy in town during October. He must have caught them in the middle of the act.

He wondered if he should change back into his pajamas and crawl into bed; let them have their fun prank and watch his "surprise" in the morning to see an army of scarecrows in his front yard. He wondered if perhaps a whole group of folks from town might be rising early to be there to see his reaction and extend their official welcome.

But he was too curious.

He wanted to see how they were doing it – particularly, how they were doing it so quickly. He thought of those exposés on the crop circles, on how a very small group of people using just a board and a rope could create intricate patterns in a wheat field, completely baffling authorities for years. Perhaps the scarecrow planters used similarly ingenious techniques.

He giggled in anticipation of what he'd learn catching them in the act as he retrieved his jacket from the front hall closet. But before he opened the front door, he changed his mind, thinking it might be better to sneak out the back door. That might give him a bit more cover, a chance to see how they were doing it before they detected him.

Wilson was methodical, analytical and studious like his father, Graham who was a steadfast engineer until the day he'd died. Wilson, of course, had loved his father deeply, and ended up taking computer engineering courses in an attempt to please the old man who'd hardly ever spoken a kind or loving word to his son.

To Graham Kendrick, being a good father hadn't been about providing a loving and nurturing environment, but about ensuring the child was provided with the proper series of stimuli and the appropriate opportunity to manipulate and explore the physical world around him. Instead of cuddles and hugs, Wilson received books and magazines. In place of loving words and encouragement, he received construction toys and computer components.

Wilson would always remember that spring when he was in grade 8 and his classmates were chatting delightedly about their summer spent playing baseball and football and going swimming and hiking and riding their bikes. That was the summer Wilson spent diligently disassembling and reassembling the Commodore Pet computer. Only once he completed that task would his father allow him the opportunity to actually use the computer and discover the programming languages of BASIC, COBOL, FORTRAN and Pascal. At the tail end of the summer, his father's treat to him, upon passing the test, was allowing him to examine the programming code of the various rudimentary games for this system.

"You'll appreciate playing the games when you understand how they work," Graham Kendrick told his son.

"But Father," Wilson moaned. "Can't I just play the game first? Just for a few minutes."

The old man simply shook his head. "Learn the code first. Make detailed notes. Once I read your notes I'll decide if you're ready to play."

The joys and wonders of creating new landscapes and environments via programming eventually captured Wilson's imagination, and despite his initial frustration, he was eventually thankful to his father for pushing him.

Of course, it wasn't until much later in his career as a programmer that Wilson realized his mother's own passion for studying and writing haiku and renga also had a deep influence on him. Renga, a form of Japanese collaborative poetry, was not unlike the discipline required when working on a piece of programming code that was part of a greater piece of software.

Wilson actually derived the name of his software company, Daisan from a renga term referring to the third stanza of a renga which allowed the next collaborative poet greater freedom. And that is exactly how Wilson had earned himself and his two partners a small fortune. Their concept of channeling shareware and open source code programming through an integrated desktop application directly linking programmers with each other to provide instantaneous wiki-like feedback from around the world was viral in its use. This shared real-time collaboration resulted in stronger, quicker generational growth in programs, and provided greater opportunities for developing programmers all over the world to become recognized by large software companies.

The rising success of Daisan led to the sale of the company to a large platform enterprise. This allowed Wilson to retire at forty-five and pursue other passions; researching his family history led him to this small eastern seaboard town in Nova Scotia, Canada, where his Scottish father had grown up and met his Japanese mother.

Of course, the other passion that led him to Nova Scotia was the beautiful Ashley; the only woman Wilson had ever loved, and who still held a central place in his heart. He'd met Ashley on his first visit to Halifax ten years earlier, and returned in the hope of winning her love. But when he arrived to learn that ship had sailed a long time ago, he focused instead on the family research.

He slowly cracked open the back door and peeked out. There was less fog in the back yard and the moonlight shone down like a flood-light in the sprawling knolls of his property.

He spotted a figure moving near the grey birch tree just a few yards away. But he realized it wasn't one of the pranksters. Instead, it was another scarecrow, its one arm blowing in a gentle breeze.

He scanned the rest of the yard. At least another dozen scarecrows were scattered about; some standing beside trees, others in the middle of the open expanses of fields.

He slipped out the door and shut it quickly.

Standing on the cement of the back-stoop Wilson breathed in the salty sea air; a habit formed quickly on his very first trip to the east coast and something he unconsciously repeated with each initial step outside.

Able to see more of the yard, and more of the figures scattered about, he realized there must be at least two dozen of the sentries standing guard back there.

Wilson again surveyed the yard for any sign of movement and listened for any noise. It was a calm, quiet night, and there was no sound of rustling footsteps in the leaves or any other indication that there were pranksters moving about in the dark. Wilson heard a car moving down the highway that ran past his house, and the distant resonance of the waves on the nearby shoreline, subtly muted by the fog. A temporary shift in the wind brought with it a strange faint clicking noise like a chorus of knitting needles. It brought to mind the image of an arena filled with a thousand grandmotherly ladies, busily knitting away. Then the noise was gone just as quickly and the night was silent.

Damn, they're good. Really good, he thought, unable to detect any movement other than the occasional scarecrow arm moving in the wind.

Confident that none of the pranksters were within eyesight, he crept cautiously to the nearest grey birch. They must have an entire barn full of these scarecrows, Wilson bemused, beginning to note the neighboring farms likely to be able to hold such an army.

When he got closer to the scarecrow near the tree he was startled to see how realistic her design was. This scarecrow was dressed like a middle-aged woman in a pale blue suit jacket with a pink button down dress shirt. She had brown wavy hair and large white loop earrings. Her face was flesh colored, some sort of latex; she had eyebrows and painted red lips and glassy bead eyes that reflected the moonlight. As he leaned in to study her face, he detected the faint scent of mothballs and thought he saw a subtle movement in her eyes he figured was the effect of a wisp of cloud passing in front of the moon.

He spent a few moments staring at this woman before he turned to see a figure a few feet to the right he hadn't noticed earlier; a man in a blue tartan shirt with a grey checked sport coat. Wilson took a few steps toward him.

The man had a large nose, grey black hair, big brown eyes and also gave off the subtle scent of mothballs. His mouth was partially opened revealing a set of pearly white teeth. How cleverly realistic, Wilson thought, reaching up and touching the man's latex face.

Wilson jerked his hand back.

The scarecrow's face was warm to the touch.

He pressed a finger onto the man's cheek and left it there.

Yes, definitely warm.

He tried to find the line of where the man's mask ended somewhere past his chin, near his neck. But he could spy no line, no edge. The warm latex disappeared beneath the man's shirt collar without a wrinkle.

Just then a cough echoed through the fog, startling Wilson.

One of the pranksters, he figured, turning to walk back to his house when he bumped into someone.

"Oufff," he stepped back to look at the figure, a tall male scarecrow in a beige suit coat and a pressed white dress shirt with billowing black hair and large dark eyes.

It had definitely not been there a moment before.

Wilson quickly panned his head left and then right, looking for any sign of one of the pranksters. "How the hell are you doing this?" he asked.

Despite the scientific and analytic approach his mind harkened back to folklore of the yūrei from his mother's culture and of which she told the best campfire ghost stories. Wilson had enjoyed the creepy tales about the white dressed ghosts with long disheveled hair but had never wasted a moment's thought believing them. He'd studied the different categories of yūrei but did so more out of a desire to understand his maternal heritage than of any particular interest in the fables.

Only the scarecrow in front of him brought to mind the goryō, the vengeful ghosts of the aristocratic class, and he subconsciously took two steps back before bolting for his back door, memories of his mother's ghost stories and the legends he'd read up on finally overcoming reason and logic.

* * *

"It's the Swamp Soggon!" Dale shouted, his voice loud over the static filled phone line.

Wilson couldn't think of whom to call other than the young man who tended to the landscaping and various other handyman jobs required on the farmstead. Wilson was a quick study but he'd never been one to work with his hands. Circuit boards were one thing, but wooden boards were an entirely different beast. Outside of electronics, Wilson's idea of a full toolbox was a roll of masking tape, a hammer and a flathead screwdriver.

"The what?" Wilson asked.

"Swamp Soggon. It's a local legend started by Angella Geddes. Up until a half dozen years ago she lived just down the highway in Necum Teuch. She told the tale of a selfish swamp creature with plans to turn all the townsfolk into scarecrows."

Wilson just closed his eyes and shook his head.

He'd needed to call someone, and so had contacted Dale. He figured the young man might have some sort of handle on the prankster's style and methodology, that he was likely to know exactly who was involved. But instead the young man was going on all half-cocked about some sort of swamp creature.

Wilson momentarily wondered if perhaps Dale was in on the hoax, a part of the prank. But he shook that thought off easily when he heard the young man continue.

Dale started rambling in a chopped and anxious tone Wilson had heard only once before from the young man. "I'd always thought those stories were a lark, something the old lady cooked up for fun, for enjoyment, to amuse neighbors, to attract tourists. I had no idea the Swamp Soggon was actually real."

As Dale continued to rave about the old woman's mythology in slow repetitive cycles, Wilson thought back to the only other time he'd heard that same panic in the young man's voice.

It had been earlier in the summer, a particularly hot day in mid July and Dale had been doing various maintenance tasks around the yard. At noon, Wilson had gone looking for the young man, bearing lunch and a portable magnetic chess set when he heard, very faintly, Dale's panicked muffled yells.

The calls had come from the root cellar, a five by eight-foot storage space partially dug into a small knoll far back on the property that you could only get into by dropping into a small ditch and crawling under the wall.

As Wilson got closer he could hear a low steady throbbing that at first sounded like an engine. Wasps. Hundreds of them. Inside the wall of the root cellar.

It took over an hour for Wilson to convince Dale to climb back down under the wall to get out, that the wasps were so busy banging against the sides of the wall that they wouldn't notice him if he was did it quickly enough.

Dale got out without a single sting, but Wilson never forgot the intense panic in the young man's voice that afternoon.

The voice he heard on the phone contained the exact same tone of alarm.

"They're going to keep multiplying!" Dale said. "The old woman was right. It's all part of the Soggon's grand plan to take over the town. You've got to get out of there. Now!"

"Dale, listen," Wilson said. "There's no such thing as a swamp creature that can turn people into scarecrows. It's a prank. An elaborate and complicated one, for sure. But a prank. I'll get to the bottom of it, okay?"

"No, Mr. Kendrick. Don't hang up! Don't go back out there! It's not safe!"

"Dale," Wilson said in as calm a voice as he could. "Listen. I'm sorry I woke you. I'm sorry to have bothered you. It's fine. It's all fine. Good night."

He placed the receiver back in the cradle and shook his head again. "Swamp skoggin' indeed," he muttered. "Or was it a soakun?" He let out a short laugh. Nothing shed the substantive light of reason on a situation more than listening to someone who had lost all voice of reason. Hearing Dale go on about the dangers of a nasty swamp monster washed all nonsense about the ghosts of his mother's mythology from his mind.

And he was even more determined to get to the bottom of how these pranksters were perpetuating this hoax. Particularly since they likely hadn't expected him to wake up and "catch" them in the act – thus their ability to remain undetected despite his ongoing investigation spoke highly of their skill at quick adaptation.

But they must have access to a convenient storage facility.

The Saunderson's barn just across the road seemed the most likely place.

Wilson put his jacket back on and headed out the front door to go have a look. The Saundersons had a teenage son. Perhaps he was involved in this with several of his friends.

As he moved through the front yard, he didn't bother trying to remain undetected. The pranksters obviously knew he was out and about and were maintaining the charade of continuing to plant the scarecrow army into their posts while remaining undetected. As he walked across the front lawn, Wilson counted another half dozen scarecrows. Among them were several children figures. Some of them weren't standing; two of them were leaning against trees, and one was sitting atop a boulder. He chuckled at one that seemed to be lying atop the roof of the shed at the end of the turn-around in his driveway.

As he crossed the highway, he thought he could hear the cacophony of knitting needles he'd heard earlier, and he stopped in the middle of the road to listen. But like before, the sound faded as quickly as it had come on and he continued along.

The fog was thicker on this side of the highway, being that much closer to the sea's edge, and it carried with it a heavier, more pervasive scent of the salty sea air. The rhythmic lapping of the waves on the nearby shoreline was also louder and offered him a sense of calm and normalcy.

Wilson didn't notice the Saunderson car in the driveway until he had traversed almost halfway up the drive and was just a few feet away from it. As he walked past the black Volkswagen Passat he noted the droplets of dew on it but still touched the hood to feel that the engine underneath it was cold. If they had gone away this past weekend on one of their regular family trips they had definitely arrived back a long time ago.

Wilson was walking past the Saunderson house on his way to the barn when he spotted a figure standing on the front porch. He stopped and raised his hand in greeting but then quickly lowered it when he realized it wasn't Eric Saunderson, but a scarecrow. He took a few steps forward.

"Well I'll be damned," Wilson whispered. This scarecrow looked just like his neighbour Eric Saunderson, complete with the red plaid hunting jacket he always wore on cool fall evenings, the horn-rimmed glasses and the distinct and particular hair patch on the crown of his head. The scarecrow had a small round circle of hair on the top middle of his head, separated from the rest of the receding hairline like some inlet island. It was a perfect match to the island of hair Saunderson boasted.

Wilson laughed, completely impressed with the detail.

But it didn't make sense to him that the pranksters would go to that much pain, particularly with this scarecrow being completely out of visual range from his own front step.

A chill ran up Wilson's spine.

There was something more amiss here than he'd been willing to admit.

A car turning the corner down the highway threw a fog blurred headlight beam across the front of the Saunderson house. In that quick flash of subdued light Wilson saw one of the Saunderson children sitting on the front step swing, or rather, the likeness of the young girl in scarecrow guise. And behind her, visible through the front window, was the likeness of Pamela Saunderson, in her blue pansy print house dress, still holding the television remote in her right hand.

For the second time that night, Wilson turned and ran back to his house.

As he ran, he held his right arm strategically over his mouth and nose, fearful of breathing in a toxic substance and tried to ignore the fact that at least two or three more scarecrows had appeared in previously vacant spots in his yard.

The phone was ringing when he got inside.

Out of breath, he stumbled to the phone.

"Hello?" Wilson huffed into the phone as he picked it up.

"Mr Kendrick?" It was Dale. "The phone kept ringing. I was scared you'd gone outside. Thank God you answered. Don't go outside. Don't go anywhere near the swamp. If you can get to your shed without being seen, here's what you need to do. You need to-"

"Dale!" Wilson interrupted, finally catching his breath. "Stop it! There is definitely something going on. I think it's some sort of airborne contagion. I've never seen anything like it, but I've formulated a quick theory. I haven't thought it through completely, but . . ." Wilson stopped talking, realizing he was rambling on in the same manner Dale had been.

In the run back to his house he determined that what he was seeing might have been caused by some airborne substance, possibly carried in from the sea on the fog. He suspected it was causing a reaction not unlike the side effects one might see with Tetrodotoxin. It made sense, given that this deadly neurotoxin was found in puffer fish and some species of marine toads and tree frogs and that the side effect was paralyses and the appearance of death. Wilson amused himself by noting it was a Canadian ethno botanist, Wade Davis, who had created a pharmacological case for zombies in his studies and research.

He deduced that the neurotoxin, which could be passed into the bloodstream through topical exposure, was somehow carried on the fog and causing the zombie-like appearance in the victims. The reason people might have seemed to appear out of nowhere on Wilson's front lawn could be due to confusion – another side effect of the poisoning – and mass panic.

All these thoughts and theories, still not completely resolved were swirling in Wilson's head when he'd answered the phone. He'd made a rash error by blurting it out, particularly to a young man without the scientific knowledge or background to understand it.

"Mr. Kendrick. Are you still there?"

Wilson took a deep breath. "Yes, Dale. I am. Now listen. There is something seriously wrong going on. You need to stay inside, keep the windows closed. And don't go out."

"But, Mr. Kendrick." Dale pleaded. "You've got to stop the Swamp Soggon. Fire will do it. Swamp creatures crave moisture. They're afraid of fire.

"There are a few ten-gallon gas cans in your shed. You can use them to dose the scarecrows then light them on fire. Burn them. Surround your house with a wall of flames. Don't let any of them, or the Swamp Soggon in."

Wilson recoiled at the b-movie antics Dale suggested; never mind that he was holding fast to some supernatural hocus-pocus theory of a swamp creature. The entire scenario he'd been suggesting was farcical.

Rather than continue with an argument he knew neither of them would budge on, Wilson thought his best course of action was to hang up and alert the authorities. Given that there was some airborne contagion, they needed to shut down the highway, establish the greater Moser River region as a hot zone.

"Dale," Wilson said. "I'm hanging up now. Whatever you do, stay inside. Keep the windows and doors closed." Dale lived several kilometers down the highway in a neighboring community, and Wilson couldn't be sure how far the contagion might have spread. With that said, he pushed his finger down on the receiver disconnect button.

When he lifted his finger a moment later Dale was still there. The young man hadn't hung up and the line hadn't disconnected.

"Dale," Wilson said calmly. "Please hang up."

There was no response on the other end.

He placed the receiver down in the cradle.

Waited a moment.

Picked it up again.

Still, dead air. No dial tone.

Dale still hadn't hung up.

Then Wilson listened and couldn't even hear the young man breathing. Maybe the young man had dropped the phone. Perhaps after having fallen prey to the toxin, a panicked thought raced through the back of his head.

"Dale!" Wilson shouted. "Dale, are you there?"

But he was again greeted with nothing but silence.

"Damn!"

Wilson repeatedly jabbed at the release button but still didn't get any dial tone. He slammed the phone back in the cradle.

Standing over the telephone, Wilson hoped against hope that Dale was okay, that perhaps the young man was just too frightened to speak, and that's why there was no answer on the other end.

And he thought about what the young man had suggested. Dousing the scarecrows in flames. Creating a flame ring.

The young man had suggested it likely as a result of seeing too many black and white b-movies about the Creature from the Black Lagoon or something; but there was a point there. If this region of Highway 7 was falling prey to a local outbreak of some sort of contagion, he wondered if dousing the victims in gasoline then setting them aflame might help prevent further spread, at least until the proper authorities in charge of disease control could get out here.

He tried the phone once more.

It was still connected at Dale's end.

***

He plucked the keys to the padlock on the shed from the key hook in the front hall then rummaged in the utility drawer of the front hall table and found the Zippo lighter. He paused in front of the cherry oak framed mirror hanging on the wall above the table and looked at himself.

This could be it, he thought as he stared into the reflection of his own middle aged eyes, now very much droopy and tired looking. Going back out there would likely mean exposing himself to whatever toxin was currently floating around in the air on the fog. And it could mean certain death.

But, understanding what he did, there was a chance he could at least slow some of the spread of this down; lead authorities to discover what was happening.

He never thought of himself as a hero, even in the fantasies that played in the back of his mind. He was a software developer, an analytical business man with a keen thirst for knowledge and answers.

And though he had fallen in love once, he'd never had a single meaningful relationship, despite decades of trying; never had kids. Sure, he'd leave behind a small legacy with the software company and products he'd developed. But that would fade in time with the emerging of new and better technologies, multi-generational versions of his products.

He at least had this. He might be able to make a difference and slow down the outbreak. Wilson thought about the two main reasons he'd moved to Nova Scotia in the first place. Initially, it was in seeking the love of a woman; but he'd also had loftier pursuits. After retiring and having enough money to do whatever he wanted, move wherever he wished, Wilson decided to move to the region of his father's childhood and research the family history.

He'd learned all kinds of details about his family, about his heritage, and had compiled a huge file of facts that he'd posted on his blog. One of the proudest was the fact that he was a distant relative of Vince Coleman, the train dispatcher who'd stayed behind in the aftermath of a collision of two ships in Halifax harbor (one loaded with tons of dangerous explosives) to telegraph an urgent warning to an incoming passenger train. Coleman had died that morning along with 2000 others in the Halifax explosion of 1917; but not before saving the 700 lives of the people aboard the train he'd sent the warning to.

Wilson figured that the least he could do would be to carry on in that proud example of nobility.

He considered the fastest and best way to both get the word out as well as alert authorities would be via the internet. So, he ran into his study to boot up his computer. A quick single paragraph blog entry would explain what he was doing in case he didn't survive to tell the tale; and an auto blast of his message via an RSS feed sent out to all his contacts via two social networking platforms in which he boasted over 3000 "friends" – mostly other like-minded computer geeks and scientific minds – would likely reach the proper authorities in record time.

With that done, Wilson went to the kitchen, turned on all of the burners on the gas stove, then ripped a curtain off the kitchen window and laid it across the burners. They erupted into flame immediately, and he tossed the burning curtain back toward the window, watching it catch the other, still hanging curtain.

He fled out through the back door of the kitchen and raced to the shed at the side of his house.

By the time he got to the shed, the flames from inside the kitchen were so bright they lit up the entire back yard, and he was easily able to negotiate the key into the padlock. He flung open the shed door and in that same light was able to find the gas drums Dale had mentioned.

As he was hauling out the first steel drum, he caught sight of a scarecrow just a few yards to the right of the shed that he hadn't noticed before.

He dropped the drum and the lighter and stared at her.

"Ashley," he whispered, not able to take his eyes off the scarecrow, mesmerized by the way the flicker of the fire light danced in her short red hair.

He took a single step forward.

"No, please don't be Ashley. Please . . ."

He took another step forward, then another, until he was standing in front of her. He put his left hand up to feel the warmth of alabaster skin. His right hand stroked her silky red hair as he stared deep into those teal green eyes and thought back to the very first night he'd lost himself in them.

It had been a decade earlier. Wilson had flown in to Halifax to attend a tech conference. On an evening out with fellow delegates, he'd ended up at The Lower Deck, a bar down on the waterfront when a gorgeous young waitress caught his eye, or rather, his ear.

He overheard her discussion with an older couple at a neighboring table as she slid two bowls of clam chowder in front of them.

"I had a chat with the chef and wanted to assure you that this chowder, our house specialty, has absolutely no shell fish content in it."

"Thank you," the man said, dipping his head.

The waitress then pulled her notepad out and ripped off the first page. "And just to ensure you're aware of the contents, I had the chef list every single ingredient he used." She handed them the paper with a huge grin, winked and gently touched the arm of the old gentleman. "Now you just keep this paper confidential. We don't want any of our competitors finding out our special secret ingredients."

Laughing, the couple thanked her and she moved over to Wilson's table and introduced herself as Ashley.

The young woman was pleasant, sweet, courteous and charming and Wilson had never seen such a lovely smile.

Regardless of the entertaining musical show and great conversation with fellow delegates Wilson found that he could not keep his eyes off of the pretty red-head. It wasn't out of any sort of drunken lust—he simply derived pleasure from gazing at her.

She'd noticed his stare early into the evening and often interpreted it as a sign that he needed another drink. Delighted to have an excuse to chat and flirt with her, Wilson continued to order rounds of drinks for the group at his table. Each time she came to the table, they exchanged short quick pleasantries and he was as enthralled with the sound of her voice as much as he had been with her cute close-mouthed smile. Through the course of the evening, she'd learned his first name and they'd fallen into a comfortable pattern of humorous exchanges.

When the bar closed and the other delegates had piled into cabs to head home, Wilson didn't want the wonderful evening to end. He was still high with the pleasures of flirting with Ashley and admiring her pixie-like beauty all evening. He'd never been particularly smooth or popular with women, so he was surprised at how calm and natural joking around with her had been. So, trying to stretch out the evening, he took a stroll on the docks to bask in the smell of the sea air, the sounds of the ships creaking in the movement of the waves, the lights of Dartmouth across the water. His hotel was at the south end of the docks, so he'd ventured north on a short stroll, exploring a bit before turning around and heading back.

Just a few yards past where The Lower Deck was, he spotted Ashley walking along the deck ahead of him. She turned her head slightly when she heard the echo of his footsteps on the boardwalk and smiled when she recognized him.

"Hi, Wilson. I didn't figure you for a stalker," she said, still smiling.

He laughed and his face turned red. "It's just so incredibly beautiful out here," he said, one arm waving toward the water. Then he turned back toward her, the beer speaking the next words. "So incredibly beautiful. Like you."

Wilson paused, realizing what he'd just done. His jaw dropped open. He'd never been so forward with a woman before, imagined what he'd just said sounded like a goofy pick-up line. He had no idea how she'd react.

Ashley smiled, then laughed. "Thanks. But you're drunk. All girls look pretty to you right now." She offered out her elbow to him. "C'mon. Take my arm. I'll make sure you make it back safely to your hotel."

He tentatively hooked his elbow around hers.

"But just to warn you," she grinned as they started walking together. "You make any funny moves and I'm tossing you right into the drink. I have a black belt in karate and Jujitsu."

"Really?"

"No, I'm just pulling your leg. But for a scrawny little chick I'm tough, and I'll lift you over my head and throw you into the water as sure as I'm standing here."

Wilson laughed. "I don't doubt for a second you're capable of it. But I doubt you'd hurt a flea."

"Not true," she grinned wryly. "I've killed plenty of fleas in my time. Mosquitoes, black flies and spiders too."

He laughed again. "You're a walking exterminator."

It was a forty-five-minute walk to the end of the boardwalk where Wilson's hotel was. Wilson soaked in the details about Ashley's life and was as impressed with her as he was with the picturesque scenery.

They couldn't have been more opposite in their backgrounds and views on life, but Wilson admired everything about her. A farm girl from a small town a few hours outside of Halifax, she'd graduated from the local University and had been working as a waitress in the evenings since her second year in University to pay for school. And since graduating, she also had a day job working afternoons at a nearby restaurant. She had at least another year of working the two jobs before she'd be done paying her student loans. Once that was done, she would take her B.A. back to the dairy farm near Moser River which her father still ran, and apprentice herself to take over the business.

Wilson couldn't fathom why someone would return to the hard and rugged routine of farm life after earning themselves a post-secondary education that could land them a better job.

But this just led to the mystique of Ashley, and what became his decade long infatuation with her.

When they were within sight of the end of the boardwalk, they stood near a large docked fishing vessel and talked for another forty minutes. The conversation hadn't even come close to running dry, but a drizzle of rain brought it to a quick end.

"It has been great chatting with you," Ashley said, her green eyes beaming. She kissed him briefly on the cheek before turning and walking away. "You're a sweet man. Goodnight, Wilson. Have a safe flight back home."

"Goodbye Ashley," Wilson simply grinned and waved goodbye as she headed toward Morris street to her apartment.

He stood there and watched her retreat, not taking his eyes off of her until she completely disappeared from view, thinking he'd never again see this magnificent woman whom he felt so naturally comfortable with. He remained motionless for another few minutes, still basking in her warmth as he stood alone on the dock, barely noticing the cold rain plastering his clothes to his skin.

For years after that meeting, Wilson wondered if the rain had been the perfect cue to invite her to his hotel room.

Of course, Wilson had never been a smooth operator and that single hour of conversation with her was the closest he'd ever come to having a relationship with a woman. Pathetic, he knew. But his heart never stopped burning for Ashley, and she had been a good part of the reason he'd decided to retire in Halifax. Sure, there'd been the desire to research his family background, but there'd also been Ashley—and Wilson often didn't make a decision unless there were two solid deciding factors to prompt him.

When he'd returned a decade after meeting her – six months ago now – and looked her up, he was overwhelmingly disappointed to find she'd gotten married five years earlier and already had a three year old son. He didn't bother contacting her, figuring she wouldn't remember him anyway, but had continued to admire her from afar, at least somewhat content to know she was happy and prosperous.

Until now.

The virus had gotten to her.

Wilson stood before the woman he'd loved and yearned for and let his tears flow.

"I loved you from the moment we first met, Ashley," Wilson said, his words wet and heavy. "And I never stopped loving you all these years."

Then he did something he'd never dared do before.

He leaned forward and placed a single gentle kiss on Ashley's lips.

Like the others, her latex-like flesh was warm.

Then he took a step back to admire her again. Even in this grotesque and creepy scarecrow form, she was as beautiful and glowing as he first remembered her. He continued to stand and admire her, never tiring of the pleasure of gazing into her eyes.

As he stared into those glassy green orbs, he saw a tear well up in the corner of her eye socket and run down her face. Imagining it was just moisture from the fog gathering there, he dismissed it, until a second tear strolled down after it a moment later.

"Ashley?" Wilson said, his words barely a whisper.

He reached forth, brought a single finger up to the tear rolling down her cheek and caught it on his finger tip. The tear was warm.

"Ashley?" he repeated. "Oh dear, sweet Ashley. Are you still alive in there?"

The strange incessant clicking noise he'd heard earlier sounded again and something sharp jabbed into Wilson's right ankle.

He yelled and stumbled backward as he kicked at the source of the pain. A black crow scampered off across the grass. Despite the fog, his eyes were able to track it as it ran, flapping its wings to gain forward momentum, all the way to the edge of the forest adjacent to his property.

That was when he noticed something strange about the trees – and since he hadn't actually looked at them before he'd not picked up on it already. But the trees seemed alive with small subtle movement, not unlike the rustling of leaves in the trees. Only, there wasn't any wind and the leaves were dark, shadowy things. As he looked at the trees, Wilson could now see they were filled to capacity with crows. Every single tree. Thousands of black birds sat in the branches.

A subtle shift in the wind brought the clicking noise to him, the sound of thousands of old ladies madly knitting coming from those very same trees.

An intense burning cold sensation, like the feeling of anesthetic running through his veins, started at his ankle and shot up his leg. He turned back to look at Ashley, and her beautiful green eyes were the last thing he saw before he blacked out.

* * *

Wilson didn't so much open his eyes as much as his consciousness rose to slowly reveal the world in front of him like some dark black stage curtain falling away.

He was standing in his back yard, at about the spot he'd been in when he took a step back from Ashley. He couldn't turn his head, his neck was stiff and tight, like he'd slept with his head at a funny angle, but he could see Ashley.

And beyond her, the other scarecrows, hundreds of them. Faintly, softly in the background, he could still hear that maddening chorus of quiet clicking.

That's when he realized it hadn't been a dream. The whole evening had been real.

He looked back and forth as he tried to move his arms, take a step forward.

His limbs were heavy and useless. He couldn't move them at all.

The virus, the disease, whatever it was, it was being spread by those crows. Perhaps generated by the crows. Wilson tried to listen to them, watch the trees for further signs of their movement.

"I didn't know."

The softly spoken words came clearly from his right, and though he hadn't heard it in ten years Wilson had never forgotten the sweet melodic tone of Ashley's voice.

"Didn't know what?" Wilson spoke without moving his lips, but his voice was clear and normal.

"How you felt about me."

"You . . . remember me?"

"Of course I do, Wilson. How couldn't I? You were a sweet guy, and I could tell you were interested in me as a person and not just trying to lure me into the nearest bed. Before you, I'd never met a man who didn't just want into my pants. How could I forget something like that?"

Wilson didn't answer, he just strained to look at Ashley from the corner of his eye.

"But you never called. I thought about you for a long time. I always wondered where you were or what you'd been up to. Of course, after time, I realized I didn't really know you – that you were just some fantasy man who'd walked into my life one evening and then walked out just as quickly.

"But thanks to you, showing me that there were sweet guys out there, it changed the way I looked at men. And I found someone sweet and genuine. My husband Robert is a great guy, Wilson. I was first attracted to him because he reminded me of you."

Wilson's vision blurred as tears welled up in his eyes. He thought of all of those lonely years of wondering about Ashley, how he'd sat around thinking of excuses to call her or look her up on the internet and get in contact with her. But he never worked up the courage to do anything.

It was only after he retired that he finally worked up the nerve to go seek her. But even then, he had the plan of researching his family history as a backup; thinking himself a fool for pursuing Ashley from the other side of the continent.

But by then it had been too late.

And now? Now, here they were, stuck in scarecrow form, partially facing one another and apparently unable to do anything but talk. Wilson felt a pang of bittersweet happiness.

"Ashley," he whispered, his voice still choked with tears. "I never stopped loving you. Never stopped longing to hear your sweet voice again, just be near you again. Talk to me. There's time now. More than enough time. So talk to me. Tell me something, anything. Please just talk to me, Ashley."

The muffled sound of footsteps on the damp leaf encrusted grass approached from behind him. But there was another noise, although Wilson couldn't quite figure out what it was.

"Someone's coming," Ashley said, hopefully. "Mister, Mister. Over here, please help us. Please."

Wilson looked and saw a single man walking in the grass, carefully avoiding coming too close to any of the scarecrow people he passed. Wilson figured out what the secondary sound was a moment later. It was the combined chorus of all the other scarecrow people calling to him for help in vain. He simply couldn't hear them, as if their voices were of a pitch too high for the naked human ear to detect.

As the man got closer, Wilson recognized him. Tall, obviously broad-shouldered even in his thick orange fall hunting jacket; a young, distinctly handsome man with short curly blonde hair and big brown wide eyes. It was Dale.

"Dale!" Wilson called out. "Over here. It's me. It's Wilson."

Even as he spoke the words, even as his cries to be heard merged with the pathetic chorus of pleas for help from the others, Wilson knew there was no point. But he couldn't stop himself from pleading, from begging.

His pleas turned to panicked yelling as he saw Dale walk over to the steel gas drum Wilson had dropped, take a quick look around, then pick up the drum and pull a lighter out of his pocket.

Despite the intensity of his own shrill screams, Wilson could still hear each of Dale's booted steps clearly as he marched toward him and Ashley and unscrewed the cap to the gas can.

As the gasoline splashed into his eyes, blinding him, the last thing Wilson heard before that final whomph of the flames igniting was Ashley's screams.

And the maddening clicking sound of the crows in the nearby trees.

From Out of the Night

Although technology dominates our world today, there still exist things that have been with us since we huddled in caves around brightly burning fires and avoided ominous shadows. Strange beings of the night become frighteningly real to us even now as we venture into the twenty-first century. Unknown things are still out there going bump in the night; a night where most of our dreams are nightmares. Scientifically, we have grown out of the dark ages, but our fears will forever remain among other frightened figures, jumping at shadows outside the cave.

And perhaps for good reason . . .

***

Mary's screech from the kitchen came to Jack over a simple, old-fashioned baby monitor. "Here they come!"

Jack was in his basement den, putting the finishing touches on another promising non-fiction book about fear and the unknown. On the shelf before him sat several of his more popular published texts: One on Bigfoot, another on the Loch Ness Monster, several on U.F.O.'s, and then the books about a popular television series featuring a pair of FBI paranormal investigators back in the ninety's.

Upon hearing Mary's voice, he leaned away from the computer, ran his fingers along the base of the keyboard and then turned the screen off. Regretfully nodding to his unfinished project, he got to his feet and headed up the stairs.

Unseen by Mary as he reached the top of the stairs, he stood silently and observed his wife peering out the kitchen window. He studied her familiar features thinking of how often he saw her but didn't really look. Her worn face gave her the impression of someone much older than her forty-three years. She stood over the kitchen counter, silent for a moment. Her expression told him her mind was racing furiously.

When their teenaged son entered the room, Mary's head swung to orient on him, her face displaying a queer blank.

He gazed curiously at his mother.

"John, the lights!"

John clicked the kitchen light off in haste. He then moved to the front door and locked it." Are they back again, Mom?"

Mary gazed proudly at her son as he locked the door. "Smart move. And yes, they're back." She twisted to look out the window again. "There go a few of them now, to Mrs. Hancock's house. Oh, and there's another two coming up the other side of the street. Oh!" She ducked. "I don't think they saw me!"

"Why are there so many of them this time, Mom?"

"Because they're growing in strength and in number. They feed on our fear and prey on the weak-minded. They coerce others into becoming just like them. And they won't be satisfied until everyone is a blood-thirsty, flesh-eating demon like they are. They won't stop until everyone has *Become*."

A burst of laughter filled the room and Mary jumped, swinging her head in the direction of the living room. A smile of relief crossed her face and Jack could tell, even before she spoke, that it had only been the canned laughter of a television sitcom audience.

"Susie!" Mary shrieked. "Turn off that TV!"

The television continued to play. Another wave of laughter from the studio audience flooded the darkened room.

Mary turned to face her son, a barely controlled panic in her eyes. "Listen, John. Take your sister and go down to the basement. Tell your father to shut off his den lights and you hide with him there. I don't want those cannibals to get anywhere near you two. Do you hear me?"

As Jack watched them, a wave of nostalgia overcame him. It was so obvious her only concern was for her children. She was willing to sacrifice herself for them without a second thought. It made Jack pine for the days when their own love had been so unselfish. But that had been years ago, before their relationship had evolved into something more mature, something increasingly less demonstrative. It was nothing like his active love for his writing. It was simply there.

While John went into the living room to get his little sister, Jack moved silently into the kitchen. His eyes met Mary's as the light and noise of the television stopped. In a thickened darkness they looked at each other and listened to their children stumble to the stairway.

"I love you," Mary whispered at their sounds in the dark. When they were gone she addressed her husband. "The kids'll be safer down there, hidden away. *They* won't have access to them."

"Why don't you go downstairs with the kids, hon?" Jack suggested. "Let me handle them tonight."

"No. I'm not defenceless. I can protect my family just fine. Now get yourself back downstairs and look after my children. They're going to need someone with them."

"Mary, please," he said, reaching out to touch her shoulder. "I can protect us."

Flinching back from his touch, Mary glared at him. "No. No, you can't. If you'd wanted to protect us, you would have put the boards up like I suggested."

"We don't need the boards, Mary." Jack thought back to the year before when she'd insisted that he nail boards on all the windows and doors. They'd stayed in the boarded-up house for three days. Fortunately, the kids were able to get an online hook up to their classrooms, so they didn't miss school. And Jack's writing work hardly had him leaving the basement den, never mind the house. So, it hadn't been that much of a hardship. But he couldn't justify using the boards this year. The nuisance was just too much this time. His manuscript was already overdue, and his agent was calling three times a day; twice less than his editor.

"Yes, we do need the boards. The boards were probably the only thing that saved us last time." She crossed her arms and paced the length of the kitchen, careful to stay out of touching distance. "What about Mr. and Mrs. Allen two doors down? They didn't board up their house last year and look what's happened to them. They're changing, they're *Becoming*. They may not be consuming flesh yet, but you can tell they've started to change. You can see it in their eyes. *Becoming* doesn't happen overnight, Jack. It has to grow and fester inside them over time. It's a horrible process of self-induced pain and suffering."

"Mary, I honestly don't think it was because of the boards. We'll be perfectly safe without them."

"You're right, the Allens were weak. Ted and Lisa just couldn't resist their supernatural charms and promises of immortality. But they wouldn't have had to resist them had they boarded themselves up inside." She peeked out the window once more. "Oh damn! We forgot to turn off the outside porch light. Quick, get the switch. Get the switch!"

Jack reached for the light switch.

"Too late!" she cried. "Too damn late! A group of them have already spotted the light. They're drawn to it like moths, Jack. Like sick, disgusting insects." She swallowed noisily and ran a hand down the side of her face. "Looks like I'm going to have to finally face them. Well, at least you and the kids will be safely hidden."

Jack stepped forward, feeling guilty. He couldn't even remember the words of comfort he used to be able to find for her when she'd needed his strength. Despite the urgency of the situation, the desperation in her voice, his mind kept wandering back to his unfinished manuscript. No matter how hard he tried, he honestly wanted nothing more than to go downstairs and continue writing.

Feeling like a poseur, he tried again. "Mary please. Go downstairs and let me handle it."

"No. You don't know all their tricks, Jack. They have to be invited in. They can only corrupt those who invite them in. There's no need for all of us to be exposed to their horrors. Besides, I'm the strongest minded. Maybe they won't be able to convert me into one of them. I should be strong enough to resist them."

"You're right," Jack sighed. She was right, too. She was one stubborn lady, impossible to sway once her mind was set. He knew that all too well. "I know you can do it. I'll go downstairs and wait with the kids. Good luck, Mary." He headed for the basement stairs.

"Wait, Jack. Before you go, promise me something."

He paused on the top step.

"It would kill me to corrupt my own family, but that's what they do, that's how they survive, isn't it? By making others like them? Promise me that if, after this meeting with them tonight, if I *Become*, you'll take the children far away from me. Promise me you'll do everything you can to prevent the kids from *Becoming*. Promise me that."

Jack took a deep breath. "I promise."

A heavy knock sounded through the darkness. "This is it." She leaned back against the counter and sighed. "I'll wait a minute and make sure you're safely hidden. I love you."

A tear came to Jack's eye. He brushed it away. "I love you too, Mary." The words rolled off his tongue like a forgotten language. He quickly moved down the stairs.

When Jack got to the den, he closed the door behind him and sat in the armchair near the computer. Susie ran over to him, jumped into his lap, and threw her arms around him. She was trembling.

Over the baby monitor, he could hear Mary's footsteps upstairs as she moved to open the door. Turning the monitor off, he frowned as he attempted to suppress a chuckle. "It's all right, Susie. It's okay. Mommy's going to be okay."

She looked at him questioningly and found courage in her father's eyes and voice. Jack was slightly irritated at how Mary's behavior had frightened their daughter. John understood what was wrong with his mother, but Susie, being four, was still too young to make sense of it.

All she knew was that mommy was scared to death of those *Christians*.

The Christians, with their non-scientific belief in life after death, resurrection of the dead, and their weekly consumption of another man's flesh and blood.

Mary was a perfect wife and mother in all other respects; so, what was so wrong in having one paranoid delusion? It was natural. In fact, Jack based his living on other people's paranoid delusions and fears. Paranoia and fear helped to feed his family. And besides, it was a simple harmless paranoia.

It's not like Mary would ever hurt anybody.

Suddenly inspired, Jack put his daughter down and told the children to watch the television in the room across the hall so long as they kept the door closed and the volume low.

He brought his hands down gently on the keyboard, and, smiling, he wrote what he felt would be a satisfying conclusion to the introductory chapter.

* * *

Irritation occurs in the true believer's heart when science or the reason of daylight find rational ways of knocking their beliefs and fears. But given the fact that proving the non-existence of anything is virtually impossible, fears continue to haunt us. We are pursued from out of the night by dreams of the unknown and visions of the unexplainable – the unreal.

Even if, one day, proof is given that our fear-created beings do not actually exist, we will probably invent new ones.

***

The doorway to the den opened, startling Jack out of his reverent typing. He looked up as Mary's throaty laugh filled the room.

"I did it, Jack," she said. "I protected my family from them. They're never going to get us now."

Mary stood in the doorway clutching a blood-stained butcher knife and smiled a bright white-toothed grin at him from beneath the coat of deep crimson on her face.

He looked at her a moment and realised the frightening truth.

There were no more monsters out there.

Ghosts, vampires, witches and bogeymen had all been vanquished. Monsters, creatures of the night and ghouls had all been conquered, and there was no need to create new ones. The only monsters left were the ones inside our own hearts. The demon thoughts that allowed Mary to obsess over something she was afraid of until the insanity finally consumed her; the spirits of selfishness that allowed Jack to simply overlook her problems because he was too busy focussing on himself and his writing.

These personal monsters that people never want to face, were the only nightmares left.

These thoughts, his most brilliant conclusion yet, would never make it to the printed page, because for the first time in eight years, Jack completely forgot about his writing as he got up, went over to his wife and held her while she wept.

Memento Mori: A Curious Nightmare
a moral tale dedicated to Mark Twain

The night before last I had a curious nightmare. Apparently, I sat on my doorstep in quiet thought with the hour nearing twelve o'clock. It was a warm evening for the last day of October, and I was relishing in the calm splendour of what might have been the last nice evening to be sitting outside so long with only a thin jacket around my shoulders.

The children, who, earlier that evening, had roamed the streets dressed in the usual garb of witches, ghosts and goblins were by then safely tucked in bed. Gone were their childish cries of excitement. There was not a sound in the air except for a slight wind through the trees and perhaps the distant passing of cars on the highway.

All was just right when, from up the street I could hear a boney clack-clacking. I turned to see what might be making such a strange noise on so quiet a night.

Around the corner appeared a figure, dressed in a moldy, torn shroud, dragging behind him a long box of rotting wood which could only be a coffin. As the figure neared I could detect the distinct skeletal features of his face from beneath the hooded robe.

Approaching my side, he paused, dropped the burden he had been dragging behind him, and sat on the edge of it. It creaked in protest as he put his weight on it. His jaw, held to his skull with the thinnest layer of sinew, began to clack as he addressed me.

"It is too bad," he said. "Too bad, indeed."

"What is too bad?" I asked. In that manner we all accept strangeness in dreams without a second thought. It never occurred to me that seeing a dead man drag his coffin down the street was an abnormal thing.

He brought a skeletal hand up to scratch his boney chin. "Most things. It is getting to be that I almost wish I had never died."

"Why do you say this? What is wrong?"

"What is wrong? Everything is wrong. Look at this burial shroud; it is now nothing but a rag. And this coffin, once comfortable, is now a rotting box that I can barely hold together. All my possessions are falling apart before your very eyes and you ask what is wrong?"

"Pardon me for saying, but I wouldn't think that, in your state, you would mind such matters."

"Oh," he said, his white boned grin sending shivers down my spine. "You have much to learn about death, my friend – much to learn about what you call my state. The fact is, I do mind such matters. There is an element of pride in death, and comfort is perhaps the only thing left to concern yourself with in the everlasting sleep of death.

"You see, in the early years of the last century, when I laid down to my final sleep, I was happy and at peace. I had myself a strong and sturdy coffin lined in the finest of silks. Above me, I boasted a polished smooth gravestone which had been adorned with fresh flowers and plants by my surviving loved ones. For a while, I was the proudest corpse in all the graveyard. It was a wonderful thing to be dead.

"But see the difference now," he said, and a ghastly expression developed on the decayed features of his face. "My grave is all caved-in, the wood of my coffin has rotted in places so badly that vermin have crawled in through the holes, not to mention the crawly bugs that have taken residence in my silks and what is left of my flesh. My gravestone, marred by time and the elements, now bows forward, as if in disgrace and threatens to fall flat in the moistened, flooded earth. And it has been years since anything but weeds and vines have graced my stone. My loved ones and descendants, who used to visit me on holidays and anniversaries, have all either died themselves, moved away or forgotten me.

"My headstone itself used to be a thing of pride, reading the simple term: 'GONE TO HIS JUST REWARD.' When first I died, it was a fine epitaph, one to be proud of, for finally, after a hard life, I would sleep in a comfortable, warm and dry place for all of eternity. But now the irony reigns strong. It's also interesting how the grave not two stones away from my own reads 'Death is the starlit strip between the companionship of yesterday and the reunion of tomorrow.' Now despite the awful state of the gravesite, at least the epitaph holds a little bit of hope for my neighbour. But are these decrepit, forgotten graves our just reward now?"

"But," I said. "You are dead."

"Yes," he replied. "Dead and forgotten. And while I lie in a mouldy, leaky box with maggots crawling through the sockets where my eyes used to behold the world, how should it be that you lie in a comfortable bed just one block away?"

Unable to answer him, I shook my head.

"Ah yes, I know – because you are alive and I am dead. You said it yourself a moment ago."

"But it doesn't have to be that way," I insisted. "Perhaps we can do something, the townspeople and I. We can work on the graveyard and restore it to its former glory. There is no need for you to leave. Tomorrow, I'll..."

But he cut me off. "No. No more tomorrows. It is too late, my friend. Much too late. You have all ignored our simple needs for too long now. We've already discussed the situation and the time is now at hand." He paused and grated his teeth in a way that made me shiver. "I have but one thing to say to you. Memento Mori."

Not understanding, I cast a confused look at him, to which he shook his head muttering how little Latin modern folks know and repeated the phrase in words I could understand. "Remember, you will die."

With that said, he pushed past me up the stairs. I turned so that I might stop him, but was amazed at how fast he could move his skeletal bones. Before I knew it, he'd entered my home and locked the door behind him. I was locked out of my own house.

The clack-clacking sound arose again, this time in a loud chorus. I turned to spy an entire procession of the dead, each dressed in similar mouldy robes and dragging their coffins behind them.

I screamed.

* * *

That was when I woke from the nightmare.

As I lay there I thought about the dream, wondering at the moral involved, and then decided that we place too much emphasis on the meaning of dreams. After all, it was probably just the result of a weird combination of food I had ingested and that book of stories by Mark Twain I had read prior to falling asleep. Why couldn't I have dreamed of meeting up with Huck Finn instead?

Shaking the sleep from my eyes, I sat up, and for the first time became aware of a presence in the room with me. The bed in which I typically slept alone was housing another body.

Slowly I turned to find myself face to face with the cavernous sockets of the dead man from my dream. A smile lit upon his face that struck terror in my heart. His skeletal hand lifted from beneath the sheet as he pointed the way out of the bedroom. "Memento Mori," was all that he uttered.

I got out of bed and reached for my bathrobe but found instead a mouldy, putrid shroud. Shaking my head, I donned the shroud and sadly moped out of the bedroom as the maggots and bugs sought my warm flesh.

My eyes downcast all the way to the graveyard, I did not bother to look at the others who, like me, were plodding their way down the street. Refuges kicked out of our own homes by the very dead we'd forgotten about, we slugged along like the poor losers we were.

Tired, I walked along through the neglected tombstones, until I found the one that read: GONE TO HIS JUST REWARD. With one last look at the night sky, I sank down into the hole.

And here is where I lie, hoping that this too is another dream from which I will awake. I'm also thinking that the next morning we should all get up and put some work into this graveyard – make it a nice, respectable place to dwell. But I'm tired now, and all that I want for the moment is to sleep.

It's a good idea though. Maybe tomorrow . . .

The Stories Behind the Stories

Many of the emails and comments I receive from readers share that they quite enjoy the "behind the story" notes I regularly add to the end of my short stories and collections of short fiction.

And so, I present here, a few insights and some background information about the inspiration or source for each of the stories you have just read.

If you're not a person who enjoys watching the special features that come on a DVD or Blu-ray disc, or the special version of the movie with enhanced commentary from the actors or director, then I suggest you simply stop reading now. Thanks for picking up this collection and reading a few of my tales. I hope you enjoyed them enough to want to read more of my fiction.

If, however, you do enjoy that "behind the curtains" peek into my fiction, then we still have a little bit of time left as we stroll along together, and I bend your ear.

About the Cover

I already wrote about the origin of this collection in the introduction. But what I didn't share there was the design of the cover. Because the stories here are all reprints, many of which have appeared in eBook format of previous books I have published, I tried to incorporate images from as many of those covers as possible.

While I didn't incorporate the cover from the ECW Press anthology that contained my story "Some Are Born to Save the World" (since I didn't pay for the rights to that), I did use snippets from the covers of the following books:

One Hand Screaming & **Collateral Damage** (Skull in Mark's Eyeball)

Z is for Zombie: ***Nocturnal Screams Vol 6*** (Skull Eye)

This Time Around (Grey Wolf (Canis lupus) Portrait)

A Murder of Scarecrows (Halloween Night)

Memento Mori (Illustration from Mark Twain's Sketches)

Three of these images are likely a bit easier to spot blended into the cloudy night sky. But can you see the other two blurred into the shadows of the city that the man in the red cape is looking down at?

About "Some Are Born to Save the World"

Originally published in 2113: Stories Inspired by the Music of RUSH, *edited by Kevin J. Anderson and John McFetridge by ECW Press in 2016.*

Kevin J. Anderson and I were sitting on the street-front patio of *The Winking Judge,* a pub in Hamilton Ontario, enjoying a couple of fine local craft IPA beers when he leaned in and told me that he was co-editing an anthology of stories inspired by RUSH.

"If you could write a story inspired by one of your favorite songs from RUSH," Kevin asked, "what would it be?"

Years earlier, the two of us had bonded over our mutual love of beer, our love of the Canadian rock band RUSH, and the adoration we both had of the Halloween season. In so many ways, the two of us were like long-lost brothers who had been separated at birth, even though, as I often remind him, he's about ten years my senior.

My mind raced. My heart raced, too. I knew that Kevin's very first published novel had been heavily influenced by the RUSH album *Grace Under Pressue*. I knew that he had already co-written a short story with RUSH drummer and lyricist Neil Peart (which I was republished in 2012), and that he had been working on co-writing the novel *Clockwork Angels* in collaboration with RUSH drummer and lyricist, Neil Peart.

And suddenly, on a warm late summer evening, on the patio of my favorite local bar, Kevin was inviting me to write a story for an invitation-only anthology collecting stories inspired by my all-time favorite band in the whole world.

I was, at first, speechless.

I just stared at Kevin, likely with the biggest, most ridiculously stupid grin on my face.

And though there are so many songs from the band RUSH that have inspired me over the years, the song "Losing It" was the first that came to mind.

But I didn't say anything about it off the bat. I wanted to think about it.

"I have some ideas," I said to him, once I felt I could get my voice under control. To be honest, I was surprised that my voice hadn't cracked, because the idea of being invited to be part of an anthology of stories inspired by the music of RUSH was extremely emotional for me.

"Good," he said. "Let me know in the next week or two, what you have in mind." Then he rhymed off some of the other songs that writers he had already spoken to had called "dibs" on. He also informed me that he had called dibs on a story inspired by the main song from the album *2112*. He would be writing the title story, "2113" and it would be a sequel that ground-breaking album from RUSH.

It didn't take long for me to reflect on the song "Losing It" some more and to adapt the sad story of the loss of a great calling in life, as told in the original song, by the writer and the ballerina. In my case, though, I imagined someone who had been called to be a hero, whose enhanced abilities were used for good; and how they might face the end of such a career.

Both Kevin, and Jen Knoch, the editor at ECW Press, the publisher of this anthology, helped me refine the raw vision I had penned into something that I am truly proud of.

In many ways, writing a story inspired by RUSH and being presented to other RUSH fans, was an incredible "bucket-list" item for this writer. And it was, of course, perfect as the lead story in this particular special collection.

I'll be honest with you. I find it hard not to cry every single time that I hear the song "Losing It" – and when I saw it performed live during one of their last tours in Toronto, Ontario, I openly wept.

About "Collateral Damage"

Originally published as a limited edition (100 copy) print chapbook and eBook in 2013.

I love to kill people.

I know this is something that horror and mystery and thriller authors get to say; because we do it on a regular basis in our fiction.

But in the writing of the character of Peter O'Mallick, I have killed real people several times. And I've even raised money for a good cause while doing it.

Peter O'Mallick is the character of a horror novel entitled *I, Death*.

He was born, like at least one of the other stories in this collection, from writing I originally did when I was in high school. Peter was created in a "freewriting" exercise that I did in Grade 10 during an English class at Levack District High School. The teacher, Gary Furhman, reserved about a half an hour once per week in English class for a time slot where students had to write something – ANYTHING – on a sheet of paper and hand it in at the end of the half hour. It could be a story, a poem, an essay, a journal. Heck, it could be a doodle or just their signature. Whatever they wanted to write. They just had to write something.

I usually took advantage of those times to write a short story. Typically, some sort of eerie and creepy *Twilight Zone* style short-short story.

One of the tales I wrote was a story called "I, Death" that was written in the form of a simple fake journal of a suicidal teenager named Peter O'Mallick who believed that he was suffering from a death curse. The tale was about 1000 words.

Several years later, when I was in University, I wondered what might have become of Peter, so I wrote a story set a few years after "I, Death" that I called "Sin-Eater." It was interesting to see what had become of him.

But even then, I couldn't get Peter out of my head.

A few years after that I was looking at how I might combine the stories "I, Death" and "Sin-Eater" into something a little bigger.

That's when I decided to blog, from the POV of the angst-filled teenager and share Peter's story. I knew how the story would start; I also knew a few elements about what would happen on his journey; and I knew the end. What I didn't know (since I rarely do any sort of detailed outline for things that I write), were many of the points, many of the characters, and many of the plot twists along the way.

For me, the thrill of writing is the discovery.

And I thought, what better way to discover than to start a story online and share it openly, not knowing where it might go.

So, in 2006 I wrote "The Online Journal of Peter O'Mallick" posted to a Blogger web-log and started out telling his story via online blog entries in January of 2006.

Here's how the first journal entry opened:

Wednesday January 18, 2006. 10:23 PM

It's over. I can't believe it. Sarah won't speak to me. It's as if she blames me for her father's death sentence.

I can't say it's a new feeling, though. It's like all my life death has consumed the people close to me. First my parents, then my best friend, now Sarah's dad.

I've been where Sarah is now, but she won't let me help her – hell, she's not even talking to me.

Ever since her father announced to the family that he had an inoperable cancerous brain tumor so far advanced the doctors were giving him a 50/50 chance of living beyond one more month, she stopped talking to me, refused to see me and ignores my phone calls.

I've been four week now. Four, long, painful, horrible weeks. I think I'm going to die. I wish I was dead, actually, like so many of the people I've cared about.

Our school's guidance counselor suggested that I start this blog in order to try dealing with it.

So here I am, typing, trying to come to terms with it. But I don't want to write about how I feel – I keep stopping and just sit here smashing my fingers down on the keyboard, smashing my fists down on the desk. I want to break something, smash something, throw my computer monitor through the fucking window.

This is bullshit.

Sometimes Peter would post daily, sometimes multiple short posts in a day. Sometimes he would go missing-in-action for a couple of weeks.

But the story rolled out and began to gain followers who were interested in Peter's dilemma.

Comments on the blog (people pretended that Peter was real and reacted to him as if he were a real person), influenced Peter. He responded to them. He even wrote about the commenters. I enjoyed the strange interactive nature of this type of storytelling.

Along the way, because Peter's death curse is a real thing, and not something he had been imagining, it seemed that almost everyone that he met fell victim to his tragic death curse. Colleagues and friends were dropping like flies all around Peter.

And then, because I was living in Hamilton, Ontario at the time, I thought it might be interesting to see if I could work with the local Literacy Council to raise money for them. I collaborated with them to host an auction where someone could get killed by Peter in my ongoing blog story.

The idea was that the winner of the auction would be written into the story, meet and interact with Peter, and then be killed by him; usually based on one of their real-life fears. I also would incorporate elements about them – their passion, their career, etc, into the tale. And they got to decide if I used their real name or a fictional one.

I ended up killing off two real people in the blog.

It was great fun.

Not just for me, but also for the people I killed, who got a special thrill out of that.

The online story went on for nine months.

Shortly after it finished, I pitched a novelization of Peter's story to a publisher who was interested in it. A number of years later, it was eventually published as the novel I, DEATH that was broken into three main parts. *Part One*: Peter's Journal. *Part Two*: POV of the novel's main antagonist reading and reacting to Peter's journal. *Part Three*: Climatic encounter between *Good Guy* (Peter) and *Bad Guy* (Brecht).

In the ramp-up to the release of the novel, I was regularly attending a conference in Niagara Falls, New York called *Eerie-Con*. It's a great little con (of usually less than 100 people) and I had the chance, over the years to meet and hang out with many great writers there, including Joe Haldeman, Larry Niven and Kevin J. Anderson. (Kevin and I bonded over our mutual love of the band RUSH and craft beer and are still good friends to this day. We usually only see one another in person once or twice a year, but we regularly text one another pictures of unique beers we are enjoying in our world travels).

Eerie-Con had a "People and Things" Auction that support this con and helped them afford having big name science-fiction, fantasy and horror authors as guest of honor.

I decided to auction off the chance to be a feature character killed by Peter in a stand-alone story that I would launch the following year at Eerie-Con as a "limited to 100 copies" chapbook.

Michael Bass won the auction. So, I met with him for coffee and gathered info about him. He was a part-time comedian, he was a huge hockey fan, he enjoyed brutally honest humor. He was also afraid of heights. I incorporated all of those elements into the story, and, came up with "Collateral Damage" a stand-alone story that takes place in a timeline between Chapters 6 and 7 of Part III of the novel *I, Death*.

I am planning a sequel to *I, Death* eventually. But I so enjoy the way that the character of Peter O'Mallick can allow me to kill real people who find a thrill in that. I can imagine that there'll be many more stand-alone Peter O'Mallick tales to write in the near future.

Perhaps he might become *your* friend one day.

About "The Zombie Whisperer"

I wrote this one in response to a call for stories about "Risk Takers" for an anthology that Dean Wesley Smith was editing for the *Fiction River* anthology series.

I remember being in Oregon and in a hotel room while attending a writer's conference while I wrote the tale. And, because I was in Oregon, and that's also where Dean was living at the time. I ended up using Oregon as the home setting for the story.

Dean didn't end up buying the story for his anthology. What I hadn't realized, when writing the tale, was that Dean did not like zombie tales. At all.

Oh well. I still had fun writing it.

Part of the fun was imagining a world in which, instead of zombies taking over and causing an apocalypse, they might become just another type of sick or infected person (or non-person, as the case might be). What if zombies ended up being incorporated into everyday America? What if people could buy, sell and trade them? What if bar owners could plant them as an attraction for thrill seekers? Because, given their condition, and that they were considered non-people because they were no longer alive, but un-dead, they no longer had individual rights.

I had fun imagining the group of daredevil asshole friends who might have wandered into a bar with a chained up zombie instead of a robotic bull. Chancie and his buddies were a group of red-neck "good-ole-boys" who were reckless, enjoyed sport and spectacle, and enjoyed berating and mocking one another.

They were a lot of fun to write. They might even be fun to hang out with for a very limited time.

But, sometimes, even when being reckless and doing stupid things, they might stumble upon something worthwhile.

Like accidentally creating an antidote for the zombie virus using saliva.

The idea for that came to me only about half-way through writing the story. So, I went back and tweaked the opening of the story to make sure that snake-handler was Chancie's profession; that allowed the concept of milking the saliva to make sense.

And, of course, because of the nature of the beast, that it was more important for Chancie to prove his friends wrong than to survive, I had to end the story demonstrating that, regardless of the world-changing accomplishment, all Chancie cared about was winning, and beating his friends.

So, while this is a zombie story, it's really just a story about a bunch of crazy risk-seeking friends continually trying to one-up each other. And accidentally saving the world in the process.

About "This Time Around"

Originally published in The Darker Woods *#2, 1997.*

"This Time Around" was a short story originally written for a werewolf themed anthology. I was trying to write a story that demonstrated what it might be like to live with the side-effect of being a werewolf, without actually having the wolf appear in the tale. This story never made the cut, but there was something about the character (Michael Andrews) that really stuck with me. So, I kept refining the story.

When a writing mentor, Sean Costello, read the story, the first thing he said to me was: "This is great! But what happens next?"

"What do you mean" I asked him. "Nothing happens next. That's the end of the story."

"No, it's not the end of the story," he grinned. "It's the beginning of a novel."

I put a lot of thought into his words and realized that, even though I had intended the story to end there, I began to wonder about who the other werewolf was and whether or not Michael would actually encounter him. I wondered a lot more about Michael's double-life, and I began to write this into a novel entitled *A*[1] *Canadian Werewolf in New York*. Based on wonderful feedback from an amazing editor, I spent a significant amount of time revising the novel, which was finally released in December 2016.

The beginning of the novel overlaps with the early AM events which are documented in this story: Michael waking up in Battery Park and the rush to get to his morning meeting with his agent. The novel goes on to explore what happens once he arrives at his breakfast meeting as well as for the remainder of Michael's day.

1. *http://books2read.com/acanadianwerewolfinnewyork*

I decided to write a sequel to the novel, which will be called *Fear and Longing in Los Angeles*, and, while that novel is still unfinished as of this writing, I did release a novella in the same universe called "Stowe Away" which takes place a few months after the events in *A Canadian Werewolf in New York*. It appeared in the 2019 anthology *Amazing Monster Tales: Monster Road Trip* which was edited by DeAnna Knippling and Jamie Ferguson.

DeAnna and Jamie have a "monsters in love" themed anthology that they are reading for, so I also plan on writing a short story closer to the length of "This Time Around" to share the "meet cute" story about when Michael first met Gayle, his main love interest.

I find it funny that Michael Andrews, the un-named narrator of "This Time Around" keeps returning to short stories a lot easier than he has to full novel-length works. Maybe it has something to do with my writing during different cycles of the moon?

About "A Murder of Scarecrows"

Sometimes a story is born out of multiple elements swirling around, collected and gathered and lovingly cared for over time. But other times a story is created in a single inspired burst of inspiration composed of multiple elements that keeps me up all night with my fingers furiously pounding on those keys.

"A Murder of Scarecrows" is that second type of story.

But first, let me break this down to give a little bit of a background in pieces, to explain this story's origin.

The Scarecrows of Necum Teuch

There's a small village in Nova Scotia about 50 kilometers (30 miles) from Sheet Harbour and a two-hour drive East of Halifax called Necum Teuch. It lies between the communities of Moser River and Ecum Secum. There isn't much to this tiny community, however it has captured the eyes and imaginations of those who drive past slow enough to behold a most unusual sight.

Scattered about the yard, garden and adjacent swamp of an otherwise unassuming white house at the edge of the highway is a small army of scarecrows.

And not just regular scarecrows, but ones that are meant to look a bit more human than most.

They were originally the creation of an Angella Geddes, who, in 1998, created and named them all (offering them names such as Aunt Mary, Captain Smith and Miss Marie Marlene). They were part of a legend she created and shared that featured an "ugly" and selfish creature called the "Swamp Soggon" who, one day, grew angry and turned virtually everybody in the town of Necum Teuch into scarecrows.

The legend and scarecrows were immortalized in a book published by Nimbus in 1996 entitled "The Scarecrows of Necum Teuch." The book explained the legend, included a scarecrow game, instructions on how to make your own scarecrow as well as a recipe for Aunt Mary's "Unspeakable" soup.

Angella Geddes continued to grow her army of scarecrows until she died suddenly in 2006. Apparently, friends, family and locals kept up the tradition and have done their best to preserve the unique characters who pepper the landscape.

I recently discovered an online article, written in 2013, by Peter Duchemin[2], that tells a little bit about his own experience meeting Angella and having a tour of her wondrous creations. It's a fun story and worth a read if you're curious for more information.

The Origin of "A Murder of Scarecrows"

Between 2006 and 2011 I worked for the McMaster University Bookstore. One of the great pleasures of this job was getting to meet with campus store colleagues from across the country at events such as the twice-yearly Campus Store Canada gatherings. In November of 2007, the CSC group met for a week in Halifax.

During a couple of free nights, I booked myself in to a few book signings, and on the Saturday night, I drove my rental car through the nasty hurricane Noel which was hitting the East Coast of Canada, to the Chapters bookstore at Bayers Lake. It was a relatively quiet night at this big box store, although I was impressed with the conviction of locals. I was quite terrified with the hurricane so close, but they seemed to be going about their business nonplussed about the whole matter.

My table was adjacent to the connected Starbucks and I ended up chatting with a barista named Ashley who enjoyed spooky tales. She picked up a copy of my short story collection ***One Hand Screaming***, and we shared a few of our favorite recent eerie reads with one another. A student at one of the local colleges, she was an avid reader and book lover. Her enthusiasm and love for books shone very clearly in her eyes.

Later in the evening, Ashley came back to the table to tell me about a place not all that far away that she thought I might be interested in. It was Necum Teuch. And it concerned the scarecrows that Angella Geddes had populated the town with. But there was something about the way Ashley told me the story that made it seem as if the scarecrows were multiplying entirely on their own.

I couldn't stop thinking about the scarecrows and this small town.

And on the drive back to my hotel, a drive in which I recall swerving on the highway to avoid a huge pile of debris that must have blown from the back of a truck in the hurricane-force winds, all I kept thinking about was how much I wanted to write about this place. For

---

2. http://theindependent.ca/2013/09/20/my-adventure-with-the-scarecrows-of-necum-teuch/

a few moments I was worried I might not make it home to write the story. (Yes, that's just how passionate I can get when a story that needs to be written takes hold. I wasn't concerned about not making it; just that I wouldn't be able to write the story swirling around in my head).

I got back to my hotel close to midnight and immediately logged on to the Internet and looked for details about Necum Teuch and the scarecrows. I found a few articles about them as well as some eerie pictures. I jotted down some notes and descriptions of a few of the scarecrows, and then begin to write the story.

As I wrote, the howling winds of hurricane Noel hammered against the hotel. I was on the ninth floor and every once in a while, I paused to look out the window at the trees being forced over in the strong winds.

I wrote about 5000 or so words before I noticed that several hours had passed. I rather love losing myself in a story so much that I lose complete track of time. I made a few notes about where I wanted the story to go and then crawled into bed at about 3:30 AM.

The hurricane ended up taking out the power in the hotel – but that only added to the wonderful sense of fear coursing through me. Ashley had also emailed me a few further details that I had asked for, as well as letting me know that her father was planning a trip that would take him through Necum Tuech within the next week, with an offer to take some pictures and send them to me.

The following night, after a fun evening out with my colleagues at a local pub, I finished the first draft of the story. It came in at about 10,000 words.

I put the story aside for about a week and then came back to it. As a thank-you to Ashley and her father Dale for the background details and help provided, I decided to change my character names to honor them. At that time, I also spent some time trying to establish Dale's character a little bit more. By the time I was finished, the second draft came in at 12,000 words. I then focused on whittling the story down and cutting out some of the extra details that didn't either move the story forward or assist with illuminating the characters.

After a few more drafts, I ended up with a version of "The Murder of Scarecrows" that I was happy with.

I still haven't been to Necum Tuech to see the scarecrows for myself. Perhaps on a future trip to Halifax I'll have time to rent a car and drive out there to Necum Tuech to see if any of the scarecrows are still there.

About "From Out of the Night"

Originally published in The Darker Woods *#2, 1997. Reprinted in* **One Hand Screaming** *by Stark Publishing in 2004.*

This particular story came to me when I was in my teens. And the first draft of this story was written some time when I was likely sixteen or seventeen.

I was in the living room and my mother was running around the house shutting the curtains and closing the front door. She was slightly panicked and, considering that I had a hyper-active imagination, I was wondering what could possibly be outside during that near-dusk time period that she was so afraid of. What evil stalked our house from outside that we had to hide and protect ourselves from?

"What is it?" I remember calling to my mom in a panic.

"It's the Jehovah Witnesses," she said.

"What?" I asked, thinking I was confused. She must have said "pack of vampires" or "pack of scary neo-Nazi punks" or something like that.

"Jehovah Witnesses," she repeated. "I don't want to have to talk to them."

Even though the threat was an uncomfortable conversation with some charismatic and genuinely well-intentioned and nice people trying to force their religion on others, the idea that there was something truly evil stalking the house from out of the night stayed with me.

That inspired me to start writing a tale where I was imagining that there might be some sort of vampiric creatures turning people into them, if only they could be invited into their homes. I mean, after all, the people who had actually been outside *had* been looking to convert people, hadn't they? I was just taking the same motif and imagining something far more sinister.

A chill ran down my spine. Always a good sign that I'm on to something. If it gives me a chill, perhaps it'll give a reader a chill, too.

But even as I was writing the story, I kept reflecting on my Mom's reaction and how it had startled and concerned me. Children often develop their own fears and prejudices from the things they learn from their parents.

What if there was a woman who was genuinely frightened, perhaps even terrified, of anything remotely religious?

How might that affect her family?

Would her family mock her? Or would they humor her? Would they tolerate her occasional lapse of reason? Or would they seek to have her committed?

The very first draft of this story was a simple tale, but as I was writing it, I realized that Mary was delusional, and so I had the husband, John, be the additional point of view to help the reader slowly realize that. In the first draft, John was downstairs watching television in the family room and she sent the kids to be with him. It was a simple tale of Mary being crazy and the relief and "twist ending" was that there were no monsters, she had just imagined them. And terrified the entire family in the process.

So, when I finished that first draft, I went back and wrote the introductory italicized text piece. It was my ode to the Rod Serling moment, when, on episodes of *The Twilight Zone*, he would walk out and provide some introductory text to the story you were about to read, and then maybe also have a few concluding words. Or maybe it was like the Crypt Keeper in those old "Tales from the Tomb" style horror comics I enjoyed reading so much when I was a kid. But in either case, I liked that element of the story. It reminded me of the many books about monsters, ghosts and other eerie phenomenon that I enjoyed reading about.

In the original version of the story, the tale ends with the italicized bit about the fact that as science disproves our belief of some monsters, we'll simply invent new ones. That was, after all, the point I was trying to make. That our imaginations will always be able to conjure up new fears.

In my second and third drafts of the story, I began to wonder a little more about John. Why would he let his wife believe the things she did? Why wouldn't he seek to get her the help she needed, the therapy, the medication, the whatever to help conquor the demons inside her?

Because it was his livelihood; that's why!

John makes his living selling books about monsters and ghosts and UFOs and goblins and demons and other paranormal creatures. It works in his favor if more people believe; so, he sits back and believes it's for the best to let her, and others, have delusions, because it helps him sell more books.

I wanted to paint him as a little colder and more calculating in that updated version. To show John as looking at his wife as an experiment that he could write about in his non-fiction books about paranormal topics.

The introductory and then concluding paragraphs were meant to be reflections of writing from the book John was working on.

And so, the original completed version of the story ended with Mary facing the religious people and John having a bit of a laugh, at her expense.

But when I submitted the tale to the small press magazine *The Darker Woods*, editor Stephanie Connolly wrote back to me and said she likely the tale, but she wanted to see a little more character development, particularly within the relationship between Mary and her husband John. She also wondered if I might introduce a real danger. What if Mary's obsession was dangerous to herself and to others? Because she thought this was a life and death situation, what would happen if Mary reacted accordingly?

The sign of a great editor is when they ask the writer just the right questions to pull even more out about their characters and the situation.

Those were the exact right questions.

I went back and added more to the relationship; made John realize the coldness of his ways.

And then I wrote the final scene, with Mary showing up holding the knife and covered in blood.

And that's the breaking point – far too late, of course – when John realizes the tragedy that he let happen because he was thinking only of himself and of his writing, and not at all about his wife and his family.

It became a much more shocking, bloody, and yet emotional ending.

Thanks to the advice of a brilliant editor.

Thank you, Stephanie!

An additional aside to this story that I find absolutely amusing, is that, though I wrote the initial story when I was a teenager – heck, Mary's teenage son in the story was the "me" I had imagined – and the re-write when I was in my mid-twenties and had only had a few short horror stories published at that time, years later, I went on to become a little bit like John, in my story.

In 2014 I wrote my first non-fiction exploration into the paranormal: *Haunted Hamilton: The Ghosts of Dundurn Castle and other Steeltown Shivers*. I was living in Hamilton, Ontario, at the time and had been inspired to write it based on the local historic ghost walks of the city. And this became the first book of true ghost stories (or "true" ghost stories, depending on your perspective) that I have penned. As of the moment I am writing of this, I have five more non-fiction paranormal books out (*Spooky Sudbury, Tomes of Terror, Creepy Capital, Haunted Hospitals* and *Macabre Montreal)*, with at least three more similar titles in the works or on the back-burner.

Though I still write and enjoy fiction, I've found a minor calling in documenting "tales told as true" about ghosts and other eerie and unexplainable events.

I did not marry a woman who was psychotic and terrified of religious people.

And I do try to balance my aspirations and love of writing with my love of family.

But at least one element of the character of John indicates an intriguing case of fictional people I wrote about becoming at least part of my own reality. So I find it intriguing that I had written about a middle-aged man penning such books, only to later become a middle-aged man doing exactly that.

About "Memento Mori"

Originally published in print in **Sulphur: Laurentian University's Literary Journal Volume III** *(March 2013), as well as online in* **Dissections: The Journal of Contemporary Horror**.

NOBODY'S HERO

The first draft of this story was written shortly after I had discovered the Mark Twain tale "A Curious Dream." Twain's story, which had originally been published in *The Buffalo Express* in the spring of 1870 was a social satire meant to expose the neglect of local cemeteries. The piece had apparently had an effect on Buffalo citizens and led to improvements being made as well as national reform.

I was fascinated by the way Twain exposed, in a satirical fashion, the neglect of local cemeteries while poking fun at the materialism inherent in society. I was quite fond of him pointing out the social posturing and sense of entitlement that existed in his day. Perhaps I was so fascinated because I imagined, if Twain thought those issues were present then, I could only imagine how he might view them today.

I enjoyed the darkly humorous way in which Twain's tale unfolded. The narrator's bizarre encounter with one of the skeletons from a procession of emigrating dead stuck with me.

I marveled at some of the questions that came to mind.

Witnessing such a thing, why would the narrator simply react so calmly? Was it because he knew, all along, that it was a dream? And indeed, in dreams don't we accept the bizarre and twisted in a matter-of-fact manner? But in any case, his nonplussed reaction in and of itself leant to the mystique to the tale.

The ending, I felt, was interesting, and served Twain's purpose effectively.

But I wanted to do more with it.

I wanted to imagine a slightly darker interpretation of what the dead might do when faced with such neglect of their resting place; and, like Twain, I wanted to inject my own nugget of a themed lesson.

Also, I wanted to poke fun at the procrastination that is inherent in our society, at the tendencies to either leave something for later or for someone else to take care of.

The tale rolled out nicely – after writing it, I had to go back and ensure that, while I wanted to follow the original tale's structure, pace and style, I needed it to have its own life and unique pulse. There was a desire to preserve the original language, but I ended up modernizing some of the phrases and expressions. I wanted the reader to immediately recognize that this was a play on Twain's original piece but also divert from that story enough to make it my own.

In a nutshell, this was a fun story for me to write.

I particularly enjoyed trying to mimic, as much as possible, the voice and style of the original piece. That can often be an extremely fun challenge for a writer.

It took me much longer to come up with a title. I wanted, in the title, to elude to Twain's original story, so that it would be clear, even before reading, that my intent was to pay homage to Twain. *A Curious Nightmare* did that for me. But it wasn't enough. I went back to the tale, pulled out the Latin phrase "Memento Mori" and used that – but I kept a subtitle in order to ensure the element of Twain's original tale was immediately apparent.

ABOUT THE AUTHOR

Mark Leslie is a writer, editor and bookseller who was born and grew up in Sudbury, Ontario, spent many years in Ottawa, Ontario and currently lives in Southern Ontario.

A bookselling veteran for more than twenty years, Mark has worked at virtually every type of bookstore, has sat on the Board of Directors for BookNet Canada and also been President of the Canadian Booksellers Association, was the Director of Self-Publishing and Author Relations at Kobo from 2011 to 2017 and is currently Director of Business Development for Draft2Digital. He has given talks across Canada and the United States, in London, Paris and Frankfurt on the bookselling, writing and publishing industry.

Mark's books include story collections, horror novels, thrillers, non-fiction explorations of the paranormal, and books about writing and publishing.

You can learn more about Mark and sign up for his newsletter at www.markleslie.ca.

Other Books by Mark Leslie

Canadian Werewolf

This Time Around[1] (Prequel / Short Story)

A Canadian Werewolf in New York[2]

Stowe Away[3] (Novella)

Fear and Longing in Los Angeles[4]

The Desmond Files

Evasion[5]

Coversion (coming)

Sin Eater

Collateral Damage[6] (Short Story)

I, Death[7]

Short Story Collections

One Hand Screaming[8]

Active Reader: And Other Cautionary Tales from the Book World[9]

Snowman Shivers[10]

Nocturnal Screams: Night Cries[11]

Short Stories

A Murder of Scarecrows[12]

---

1. http://books2read.com/thistimearound
2. https://books2read.com/acanadianwerewolfinnewyork
3. https://books2read.com/stoweaway
4. https://books2read.com/fearandlonginginlosangeles
5. https://books2read.com/evasion
6. https://www.draft2digital.com/catalog/64813
7. https://books2read.com/ideath
8. https://books2read.com/onehandscreaming
9. https://books2read.com/activereader
10. https://books2read.com/snowmanshivers
11. https://books2read.com/nightcries
12. https://www.draft2digital.com/catalog/202145

Spirits[13]

Anthologies (as Editor)

Campus Chills[14]

Tesseracts Sixteen: Parnassus Unbound[15]

Fiction River: Editor's Choice[16]

Fiction River: Feel the Fear[17]

Fiction River: Superstitious[18]

NON-FICTION: Paranormal / Ghost Stories

Haunted Hamilton[19]

Spooky Sudbury[20]

Tomes of Terror[21]

Creepy Capital[22]

Haunted Hospitals[23]

Macabre Montreal[24]

NON-FICTION / Writing & Publishing

The 7 P's of Publishing Success[25]

Killing It on Kobo[26]

An Author's Guide to Working with Libraries and Bookstores[27]

---

13. http://books2read.com/spirits
14. https://books2read.com/campuschills
15. http://books2read.com/tesseractssixteen
16. https://books2read.com/editorschoice
17. https://books2read.com/feelthefear
18. https://books2read.com/superstitious
19. http://books2read.com/hauntedhamilton
20. http://books2read.com/spookysudbury
21. http://books2read.com/tomesofterror
22. https://books2read.com/creepycapital
23. http://books2read.com/hauntedhospitals
24. http://books2read.com/macabremontreal
25. https://books2read.com/PUBLISHINGSUCCESS
26. https://books2read.com/killingitonkobo

Watch for more at Mark Leslie's site[28].

Mark can be found online at www.markleslie.ca[29] and on Twitter (@MarkLeslie)

Sign up for Mark Leslie's author newsletter[30] and receive a free eBook.

27. https://books2read.com/workingwithlibrariesandbookstores

28. http://www.markleslie.ca/

29. http://www.markleslie.ca

30. http://markleslie.us4.list-manage.com/subscribe?u=ed5625948004c11696c7313a3&id=f9caf5a705

Did you love *Nobody's Hero*? Then you should read *Obsessions: An Anthology of Original Fiction*[31] by Mark Leslie et al.!

[32]

Webster defines "obsession" as an "a persistent disturbing abnormal preoccupation with an often unreasonable idea or feeling."

Obsessions sometimes include a hobby or collection that has gotten out of hand. Other times an obsession can drive a person to invent something new, cure a disease or attempt to right a great wrong. And at other times, obsessing can send a person down a dark and disturbing path.

---

31. https://books2read.com/u/meew5g

32. https://books2read.com/u/meew5g

Obsessions can be healthy; can be born out of love and the desire to protect. They can stem from a need to fix something that is broken or replace something that is missing. But they can also be pervasive and disgusting, unhealthy and bizarre. They can be mild or quaint and eclectic, or they can be all-consuming and life altering.

These authors tackle the subject with all original genre-bending fiction:

Ezekiel James BostonStephen CouchJoe CronLeah CutterDayle DermatisRobert JeschonekKari KilgoreMichael KingswoodKate PavelleAnnie ReedKristine Kathryn RuschLeigh SaundersRebecca M. SeneseDean Wesley SmithDavid StierJulie Strauss

Stories curated by Mark Leslie, editor of **Campus Chills**, **North of Infinity II**, **Tesseracts Sixteen: Parnassus Unbound** and multiple volumes in the **Fiction River** anthology series. Foreword by *New York Times* and *USA Today* Bestselling Author Kristine Kathryn Rusch.

www.ingramcontent.com/pod-product-compliance
Lightning Source LLC
LaVergne TN
LVHW090954080826
845145LV00003B/1000

* 9 7 8 1 9 8 9 3 5 1 0 9 3 *